UNFORSAKEN

~ *A Christian Fiction Novel*

Shakira R. Thompson

BELIEVER'S CHOICE
MEDIA

Believer's Choice Media
P.O. Box 2131
Yulee, FL 32041
www.shakirabelieves.com

Unforsaken
Book Cover Designed by: Gad Savage, Elite Cover Designs

Library of Congress Congress Control Number: Applied For

ISBN: 978-0-9906725-7-9 (p); 978-0-9906725-8-6 (digital)

Scripture quotations are taken from the *Holy Bible*, *King James*, *New International Version*, *New Living Translations*, *The Amplified*, *Message*, *and Common English Bible Versions*.

Publisher's Note: *Unforsaken* is a work of fiction. All characters and places appearing in this work are fictitious. Any resemblance to real persons, living or dead, places, establishments, events, organizations, and/or locations is purely coincidental and a product of the author's mind.

First Printing, 2015

To my beautiful grandmothers, Leatta and Eliza, I miss you dearly but I know your spirits live on

———————

ACKNOWLEDGMENTS

When I was growing up, I remember singing a song by the Reverend Milton Brunson called, "God's Got It." At the time, there was a young lady by the name of Alexis Tunsil, she's Alexis Tunsil Wright now but when I was younger, no one and I mean no one could sing that song like her. Alexis would start the song out, "I once was young but now I'm old but I've never seen the righteous forsaken, nor his seed beg for bread."

Growing up, I used to love that song, I still do actually and especially if Alexis sings it. Little did I know, many years later, I would write a book with that same message. I've now lived long enough to know that trusting God will allow you to know without hesitation that whatever you need, God's Got It. I've been through enough in my life to know with an assurance that I've never seen the righteous forsaken nor have I seen his seed begging for bread.

I didn't get a chance to write as many books as I'd planned this year but I'm grateful to God that I was able to write this one. With that, I need to first thank and acknowledge my Heavenly Father for granting me such a gift and talent to write what's in my heart.

As always, I have to thank my husband, Keith M. Thompson and the two little ladies who call me mommy. Without their support, I couldn't do this at all. They understand what it means when I say I'm going into the "dungeon," they know that means I am not to be disturbed. I appreciate their patience in understanding that in order to write, they may miss a home cooked meal and have to order out. I'm grateful for their support when they don't make me feel badly for piled up laundry. I'm thankful you all love me enough to allow me the opportunity to share these stories.

To Gad Savage, thank your putting up with me and my crazy demands for graphics. You are a blessing and we are stuck together now, forever.

I have to give a huge thank you to all of the beta readers who take out the time to read the review copies. I have to give an extra-special thank you to three young ladies who I love dearly, Genine Adams, Samara St. Hilaire, and Tonya Blanchard, you ladies are awesome and I thank you for helping me to be a better writer.

To the "Shakira's Sweethearts," and especially the U.S.G.I.R.L.S. book club, you all are amazing and your support means the world to me. I appreciate all of the messages of encouragement and not only that you all keep me accountable to the gift God has given me.

With this particular project, I have to thank Karla "Kay Jay" Clark for writing Cherie's song, a song that will speak to the hearts of so many people. For being a sister in Christ and working so diligently with me, I pray for God's choice blessings to be upon you and over take you in all you set your hands to do.

To my family, my parents, my sister and her family and to everyone who love and support me and to even the ones who don't, I thank you and appreciate you all so much. I mean it when I say, I'm truly grateful.

It is never my intention to forget anyone but if I have, it's not on purpose, I love you all and may God bless!

Prologue

"I didn't want to do it; I just don't know how my life has come to this."

Forcing his zipper jacket up, Carson continued, "I was once a good guy, I started off on the right track. Man, but now, my life is all jacked up right now and for the life of me, I can't figure out how it all happened. What I can remember is this idea that keeps coming in my mind is as a boy in church, I wanted to be just like my dad. Back then, that's what he was to me, my dad. I'll never forget how me, Christian, and Cayden-James used to sit behind him and mother while sandwiched in between two armor bearers and we'd stand in awe of him. Bishop had and still does a way of commanding the attention of a room and I wanted that too. When I tell you that I wanted to be like that man; I used to dress like him, I wanted my clothes to match his...I would even have my hair cut just like how he wore his."

Combing his hair neatly in place, Carson looked up and said, "I remember how I couldn't even speak in tongues but if Bishop would direct the church, "Speak in your heavenly language," from the pulpit, I would do it. I used to laugh under my breath because I knew I was babbling and stammering but on the flip side hoping and wishing God knew what I was trying to say. Nowadays I don't feel like God wants to hear anything from me. Sometimes, I feel like He's just given up on me. Hell, I've given up on me. I'm the biggest hypocrite alive."

The air in the bedroom was stale, there hadn't been much activity at Carson's home, yet he continued to carry on with life as if nothing was going on...only that wasn't the case.

Putting the finishing touches on his outfit, he thought back on how beautiful his mother, Regina would look each and every service, he dreamed as a child of having a wife and supporter in ministry like his beloved mother. However, that dream was shattered, he had neither. In less than two years, he'd not only lost his mother but he'd also lost not one but two wives, Scarlett and Rebekkah. The two women he thought were supposed to carry the promise, his legacy.

"What was I to do?" Carson asked.

Explaining further he shouted, "I mean, she came to me, telling me all sorts of things about him. I can still see the look in her eyes. I'm trying to tell you I had no choice; I had to do what needed to be done."

Trying to calm himself down, he said, "Okay, I just need to chill and see how all of this is going to play out. It's done now and that's that...it is what it is and I'm ready and prepared to let the chips fall where they may."

Not yet convinced, Carson said once again softly, "Hmm, and to think, I was supposed to be the Pastor of Wondrous Works by now and now look at me. I guess when a person feels like they have no hope, nothing to lose, or backed into corners, they don't really think about things or consequences their actions may cause. All I can say is, I did what I felt like needed to be done for my family. If this back fires on me, I'll only have myself to blame."

Rolling his carry-on luggage down the stairs, Carson locked the doors of his home and left. He was alone, the entire conversation he'd just had was with himself in the mirror.

Chapter 1

"Why are you pacing the floor like that missy? You are going to wear a hole out in this nice, beautiful flooring if you keep doing that girl, now what's going on with you?"

Wringing her hands, Cherie stopped pacing for a brief moment and started again, "Oh Grandma Montgomery, I'm sorry...I'm not real sure what's going on or what to do right now. Have you seen or talked to Carson lately?"

Shaking her head slowly, Mother Montgomery answered, "No, I haven't seen much of him lately. In talking with his father, that boy has got a lot going on with him right now, I just pray he sits himself down for a while and get his act together. Why do you need him so?"

Trying to conceal the real reason, Cherie quickly tried to think of one, "Oh, I mean, yeah, I heard about all the drama he has going on and I wanted to make sure he was alright, you know what I mean? I just haven't heard from him since the last time he and I spoke."

Mother Montgomery was no fool, she could clearly see Cherie was lying but decided to play along, "Uh-huh, yeah well I think we all could stand to sit down a while and get ourselves together, you know what I mean Cherie?"

Feeling a bit uncomfortable under Mother Montgomery's stern stare, Cherie rubbed her forehead as if to ward off the throbs of a pending headache and said, "I think I understand what you mean Grandma Montgomery, that's exactly why I came home for a while."

Nodding her head, Mother Montgomery said, "Is that right Cherie? I thought you were sticking around because of that little war you have going on with that Blue boy and now I see they talking about he might be dead."

Whatever warding off Cherie was trying to do didn't work, it felt like a lightning bolt struck her head and the roar of Mother's words sounded like thunder in her ears.

Offering a nervous laugh, Cherie had difficulty speaking and when she was able to get the words to come out they were choppy, "What do you mean Grandma Montgomery, what are you talking about?"

"Little girl, don't play with me...Mother has her accounts. I does tweet, twat, and twit, I do all of that stuff and I've been seeing what's been happening. I be on Spacebook and I be doing it for the gram. I catch up on scopes to sometimes; I think I might do a prayer-a-scope. Now, I haven't seen much on those three about this mess. Now the question is, what do you know about that boy being dead? Have you heard anything about his death and more importantly, do you have anything to do with it?

Vigorously shaking her head, Cherie yelled, "Please stop it with your crazy talk, you getting old woman. Senile, I tell you...just senile. And please for the love of all who enjoy social media, stay off of the Internet."

Raising her fist in the air, Mother Montgomery warned, "Old huh? I ain't too old to whip your tail, I can tell you that and I got your senile, child. That's what's wrong with you now, Regina wouldn't spank your little hip when you were a child. She should have cut that butt right on up. I used to tell her all the time, a swat on the rump never hurt nobody. But no, Regina was always trying to overcompensate and spoil you because of your mama."

Realizing she could no longer act in front of Mother Montgomery, Cherie conceded, "Okay, I'm sorry but I swear to God and on Auntiemama Regina's grave that I had nothing and I mean absolutely nothing to do with his death. Right now, we don't even know if he's really dead, it could be just a rumor. I haven't seen any news reports, no one has called me, and I haven't heard from my manager so I'm thinking it's all a rumor."

Standing up from her favorite, high-backed chair, Mother Montgomery said, "Now don't you dare go trying to bring God and my dear sweet, may God bless the dead, Regina into this. You are in this because of all your mess, don't do it, don't try and bring them in it...you just messy. I know what you've been doing, yes ma'am, I sure do. I knew something was up when you first came back home. Now listen here, if you are in any kind of trouble, you better go on down to the police station and see what may come of your fate."

Stepping back and rolling her head, Cherie snapped at Mother Montgomery, "And why would I do that? Plus, not only that, I haven't seen Blue since my last tour ended and I came here which is where I've been the whole entire time. You know that, you've seen me stay in this depressing house since I came back. Besides, whatever social media squabble Blue and I had is not enough to implicate me in his pretend, so-called death."

Maintaining an even tone, Mother Montgomery said, "You real high and mighty acting for someone who might be about to go to jail."

Cherie's forcibly calm demeanor started to fall apart although she tried to keep it together, "I don't know why you insist on trying to make me be a murderer, I'm not going to jail. I tell you what thought, this situation makes me feel like I'm already in jail...Geesh. Grandma Montgomery, have you ever felt like you allowed the devil to take you further than you ever wanted to go? Everything all started out as harmless fun and then quickly things started getting out of hand and I didn't know how to stop it and to be honest I don't know if I really wanted it to stop."

Mother Montgomery looked Cherie squarely in the eyes, "Well of course I have, you don't get to be my age and haven't had a few run-ins with that old rascal. But that's the deal with sin baby, it feels good. It wouldn't be hard to give up if wasn't appealing. The problem comes in when you think, oh doing this won't hurt me and you start off small and before you know...wham, bam, yes ma'am you are now caught up. He lost in place in heaven and he's trying all he can to get you to lose yours."

Despite trying to put on brave front for Mother Montgomery, Cherie's insides were turning into liquid Jell-O and melted chocolate, truth be told, she was beyond scared. Her bitter disputes with Blue on social media had become that of a fire storm when he started dropping hints about their video. He was now wanting money and every time she would agree to his amount; he would counter with a higher one. By this time, Cherie was the only one within the group of people filmed to have enough money or close to a family with enough money to meet his demands. However, she was getting tired of the games he was playing with her by holding her career and ministry hostage with that one single video.

Looking through the draped windows, Mother Montgomery said, "Well maybe that's what you think, but the police must think otherwise because they are pulling up now."

Dropping to her knees in the praying position, Cherie begged Mother Montgomery to tell them she wasn't there and to find out what they wanted.

"You think I'm going to lie for you? I'm too old to be lying and missing heaven for you, child."

With her arms wrapped around Mother Montgomery's feet, Cherie pleaded with the matriarch of the Montgomery family, "Please, please, I promise I'll get myself together like you said after this, just please if they ask for me, tell them I'm not here."

Before Mother Montgomery could respond, the doorbell rang.

Cherie hopped up from the floor and in a flash was up the spiral staircase and in her room.

Mother Montgomery opened the door with warm greeting, "Hello officers, how can I help you today?"

"Hello ma'am, do you mind if we come in?"

Opening the door for the two officers to come inside, Mother Montgomery said, "To what pleasure do I owe of your presence all the way out here gentlemen."

Chaplain Prather spoke up, "You may not remember me but I came here the night Lady Regina was killed, I was one of the officers to deliver the news. We normally don't do this but because of the deep impact she made on the lives of the community, we wanted to come by and check on the family and see how everyone has been making out since her untimely passing. We also wanted to let you know there are plans to have that road renamed after her. Is Bishop around, I'd like to talk with him?"

In a way, Mother Montgomery felt a bit of relief, she even let out a small sigh and answered, "I'm so glad you all came by to check on us. It has been a difficult time for everyone but with the help of the Lord, we are trying to manage. Unfortunately, Bishop isn't in at the moment but I'll be sure and let him know you stopped by."

Mother Montgomery's speech about the time since Regina's passing was a complete understatement. Courtney and Christian were now settled in New York, Bishop Montgomery was hardly around, he'd temporarily allowed his brother, Claude to take over as Senior Pastor of Wondrous Works, when he was home, Cayden-James only hung out in his room, and Carson rarely stopped by. To say they were managing could be subject to one's interpretation.

Not two seconds after the door shut was Cherie running down the stairs, "What did they want? Were they looking for me? Is Blue dead?"

Walking into the kitchen, Mother Montgomery didn't answer, she only kept sashaying across the floor.

Following behind closely, Cherie continued on with the questions, "Why won't you answer me, are they looking for me, am I going to jail, what did they want? Answer woman."

Putting on a kettle of water, Mother Montgomery turned and sat down at the table and pointed at a seat for Cherie and said three words, "Tell me everything."

Chapter 2

"Bishop, I have to say, I have enjoyed seeing you smile lately."

Bishop Montgomery offered up a wave of his hand, "Now Dottie, how many times do I have to tell you, I've told you to call me Eugene. Stop it with the Bishop talk, our families go back a long way, you knew me as Eugene before I became a Bishop."

Smiling widely, Dottie responded, "Yeah, I know...I guess I just forget sometimes."

Smacking his lips, Bishop interjected, "And if I'm smiling it has to be from all this good cooking you've been feeding me."

Bishop and Carson were once guests at The Bolt but Carson checked out early and Bishop Montgomery checked out shortly thereafter. However, even though he was back home, Dottie issued Bishop Montgomery an invitation to come back anytime for tea, coffee, conversation, or whatever he needed. Hoping to see Delores at some point, Bishop obliged Dottie.

Dottie laughed with a gleam in her eyes saying, "Well after the way you attacked your plate that first evening you stopped by, I knew I needed to keep you coming back for more."

Bishop's demeanor changed slightly, his muscles loosened, "Well considering the fact every time Clarice now prepares a meal she bursts into tears because Regina is gone it kind of takes the fun out of eating...if you know what I mean. Things at my house are crazy and coming out here makes me somehow feel better about myself...better about life. It's beautiful out here."

From Bishop's bowed spine and lowly chin, you could easily tell he was still mourning the loss of his wife. Since she'd gone on to be with the Lord, he was often caught between a rock and a hard place. Many times he now lived with an inability to see where his future might be headed. He had no real direction.

Noticing a shift in his mood and a change of energy, Dottie tried to bring Bishop back to a smile. Rubbing her hands together, she teased, "I have your favorite ready."

A pat to his stuffed belly showed he didn't need anything else to eat but there would be no way he could resist to his favorite dessert, baked beignets with strawberries and whipped cream.

"Oh Lottie Dottie, you spoil me, I don't deserve your kind generosity."

"It's my pleasure Bishop...I mean, Eugene. Excuse me while I get it all together."

While waiting on Dottie to return, Bishop stood up and looked around the grounds as far as his eyes could see just as he would do every time he was there with an expectation he'd somehow see or run into Delores and yet again, nothing. Looking out over the vineyard, he wondered, *"Why is she avoiding me? I'm sure Dottie has been telling her I've been out here. I just want to talk to her and I don't understand why she won't call me back?"*

"I hope you've saved some room because here you are sir, your favorite," Dottie exclaimed.

Having eyes bigger than his stomach, he smiled and said, "Yes, my favorite and I know I'm going to enjoy this."

Happy to serve Bishop, Dottie was relishing in the moment of making him happy when he smoothly changed the subject to the topic of her sister, Delores.

Taking one last bite, he said with a full mouth, "Why doesn't she want to talk to me? You're her sister, you must know. Is it something I've done?"

While she wanted to roll her eyes, a rolling stomach was all Dottie could muster in order to keep her true feelings from showing, she thought, *"I guess at some point I knew he'd ask about her but she doesn't want anything to do with him, she flat out told me that, which means he's open game for anyone, including maybe me, we are too old for any type of girl codes."*

Delores and Eugene may have been an item back in the day but Dottie always held a torch for C.E. Montgomery. He was her first crush and she was heartbroken when he chose to go out with Delores over her. She always wondered what was it about Delores that made him choose her considering they looked exactly alike.

Trying to clear the dishes, Dottie stood up and grabbed his plate, Bishop put his hand on hers and said, "This can wait, I want to hear what you have to say."

Of all the days he'd been coming there and Delores was nowhere to be found she happened to be walking through the dining room and saw them sitting out on the terrace with his hand over Dottie's.

Immediately, Delores questioned herself, *"What is he doing here and why is he holding hands with my sister? Hmmm, they look mighty cozy together. Why hasn't Dottie said anything to me about this? Should I go out there? I know we're older now but doesn't she know anything about female rules?"*

Settling down back into her seat, Dottie issued a snort of dismissive laughter, "Simply put, she doesn't want you. She's says you are a part of her past and she'd like to leave you there...in the past."

Dottie's words stung, he wasn't expecting to hear her response. He thought back to the time Delores abruptly ended things with him and in a way, he felt rejected all over again. Processing Dottie's explanation, he thought, *"I just wanted to talk and I don't understand why she would go to such extremes by trying to avoid me and saying things like she doesn't want me. It wasn't like I was asking for her hand in marriage, my wife just died for crying out loud. Women...I tell you."*

Pushing back from the table, Bishop stood up, clearing the napkin from his lap, "Dottie, as always, dinner was superb but I must be going."

"Must you leave so soon?"

Unhappy about what he'd heard concerning Delores, Bishop felt he needed to leave. Appreciative of Dottie's hospitality, he clasped his hand in hers and gave a light squeeze, thanking her.

"Indeed I must, the time for me to go has arrived but I'm most grateful for all you've done for me."

Stepping in closer, she said, "You sound like you are saying good-bye. You will be by tomorrow, same time, right?"

"I don't know Dottie; I believe all good things must come to an end isn't that what the old cliché says. I've burdened you enough as it is."

Dottie was holding onto an old cliché of her own that the way to a man's heart was through his stomach and she wanted to continue being in the company of Bishop and feeding him was the way to do so.

Still holding onto his hand, Dottie lowered her voice and said, "You've been no bother at all, I love having you around."

Dottie clearly wanted to show the differences between herself and her sister, she wanted Bishop to know that Delores may not have wanted to revisit their past but she was ready and willing.

Bishop Montgomery might've been new to being single again but he knew when a woman was trying to throw herself at him and his radar immediately went off.

Taking a step back, he dropped the hand holding moment and said, "Like I said, all good things come to an end. I appreciate all you've done for me; your kindness is not lost on me. According to the word, I pray as you have welcomed a prophet that you receive a prophet's reward[1]. You be blessed, alright. Now you have good evening and we'll talk soon."

After receiving a pronouncement from the word of God what was left for Dottie to say other than, "Okay Eugene, get home safely and I'll check on you tomorrow."

He walked quickly to his car.

Delores stood watching from her bedroom window as he pulled off.

---

[1] **Matthew 10:41**: *"If you receive a prophet as one who speaks for God, you will be given the same reward as a prophet. And if you receive righteous people because of their righteousness, you will be given a reward like theirs."* (**NLT**)

Chapter 3

"This can't be happening."

The boom of James' fists blasted throughout the entire house as if it were in high-definition surround sound.

Speaking through clenched teeth, James boiled over saying, "I knew it and I told you. How could you be so st...."

Dropping the papers onto the bed, in a huff, an indignant Scarlett yelled out, "James, you need to calm down. But wait, what were you about to say, so what James, so stupid...is that what you were about to say? So you think I'm stupid now and you think telling me I told you so is the smartest thing for you to be doing right now."

Taking a step towards Scarlett, turning his head up to the side as if to change the course of the conversation, James said, "I wasn't going to call you stupid Scarlett. However, you are probably feeling that way all on your own and I'll tell you one thing, lashing out on me isn't going to help."

"James, are you crazy or something? I can really do without the back handed comments you're throwing at me right now. It's bad enough I'm still shaking from being served."

Revving back up, James shouted, "You want me to be sensitive to your needs and watch how I talk to you when the custody of our son is now in jeopardy...all thanks to you. Now, I find myself wanting to ask, are you crazy or something."

Popping antacids one after another, Scarlett screamed, "You have to remember this, James, you were right there with me the entire time, you even pulled up a picture of the baby and showed it to Carson so I didn't do this all alone."

"Are you kidding me Scarlett; you want to put that on me? Yes, I did that but you were staring at me like a deer in headlights looking for help, so yes, I did pull up the picture but you knew how I felt about that fool. Anyone who will do what he did to you doesn't deserve to walk the earth as far as I'm concerned."

"I'm sorry James, he looked me in the eye, he told both of us he wasn't going to cause any more problems and now he serving me with papers."

Shaking his head, James scoffed, "And now you are surprised he lied? Give me a break Scarlett, will you please wake up."

Scarlett and James were getting ready to attend a birthday party at her parent's home when they were interrupted by a process server.

Lowering his head, James said, "You don't want to hear me say I told you so but you need to hear this Scarlett. I begged you not to tell Carson about Chandler. I told you I would support you in whatever decision you made but you know I was against you ever going back to California and you not only went once but twice. I thought it was a mistake to trust him with that information and I wasn't the only one, Minta told you the same thing and now look. As you can see Scarlett, this doesn't just impact you. This guy is trying to take our son after he said he wouldn't. He doesn't understand that biology doesn't make you a dad, it makes you a sperm donor and that's what he was and still is, Chandler is my son, our son."

Attempting to position herself in the fetal position on the bed, Scarlett was unable to because her little baby bump was preventing her from doing so. Still, she laid on the bed the best way she could pinning her arms against her stomach in an effort to protect the baby growing inside of her. As long as this baby was inside, she could protect them from all of the evils in the world. The evil now presenting itself again went by the name, Carson Eugene Montgomery.

Muttering tearfully to herself, in the back of her mind, she knew James was right. Replaying the moment, she decided to tell Carson about Chandler in California, she tried to reconnect to the feeling that led her to trust Carson with such precious information considering what he'd done to her. The more she thought about Carson saying he'd never challenge her for custody and seeing now how he lied, the more she became sick to her stomach.

The weight of her culpability kept her from lifting her head fast enough to make it to the bathroom and she vomited all over her bed and her husband's feet. His brand new shoes...ruined.

As angry as he was, it pained him to see his wife in the state she was in. He wanted nothing more than to protect his family and provide for them and now they were in a position where his ability to protect was in question. As a man, he felt helpless, he was afraid of what might happen and for James that wasn't a good feeling.

James reached under Scarlett and lifted her up from the soiled bed and sat her down on the chaise lounge a few steps away. Stepping out of his shoes, he walked into the bathroom and walked out with a warm towel and Scarlett's robe. With careful and tender affection, he cleaned off his wife and removed her clothes and placed her robe around her ever expanding frame.

With a whisper, James said, "You need to rest. I'll let the family know we won't be making it tonight." Kissing her on the forehead, James pulled the covers from the bed and left the room.

James' loving hands had calmed his wife, Scarlett was lying down resting while James was in the wash room. For a moment, the room was peaceful unfortunately, that moment was short-lived. Within seconds, Scarlett jumped up looking for her phone, "I need to call Bishop, better yet, I'll call Rebekkah and find out what's going on, maybe they'll be able to tell me why Carson is doing this."

Searching the room, Scarlett picked up her phone from the night stand as James walked through the door, "Scarlett, honey...what are you doing, I thought you were supposed to be resting."

Bringing a shaky hand to her forehead and looking through her phone with the other hand, Scarlett said, "I know honey but, I was just thinking that maybe if I call Bishop or Rebekkah then maybe I could try and find out why Carson has decided to do this."

James' muscles quivered, his nostrils flared as his face turned a shade of unknown crimson. Snatching the phone from Scarlett's hand, through curled lips and slow and steady breaths, James declared, "Scarlett, I've about had it with you. Get somewhere and sit down because you're done here, you've done enough already. I'm taking over this ship. See, when we left California I didn't have a good feeling about this whole situation, I've never trusted Carson to do the right thing so when we returned I contacted my lawyer. I've had him on retainer for this very moment we are faced with right now. While I was downstairs I called him and he's in the process of drafting a response as we speak. So when I tell you to chill out...I mean it Scarlett. This man thinks he can just come in and try to destroy my family, well I'm not having it."

Sitting up on the chaise and rubbing her stomach, Scarlett wiped the tears falling from her face and said, "I just feel like I should be doing something to fix this."

With his back facing Scarlett, James pulled at his collared shirt baring down on his teeth and said, "Trust me, you've done enough. You need to remember you are six months pregnant and you need to know I'm not going to let anything happen to any of you. I'm going to take care of this Scarlett, you let me handle Carson."

Chapter 4

"Something isn't right; I wonder what's going on."

Shaking his head while putting on his shoes, George asked, "What are you over there rambling about now Minta?"

In a dismissive tone, Minta walked past George and said, "I wasn't really talking to you George, I was talking aloud to myself."

"You know they have a pill for that, for people who talk to themselves, is it time to get you a prescription?"

With a hand on her hip, Minta said, "You want to crack jokes at a time like this, really George."

Rolling his eyes, George replied, "Oh Lord, what's wrong with a little jokey joke, huh? I mean, we are getting ready to host a party in a little while and you know what there is still some time before everyone gets here."

A glimmer of light shown from George's eyes as he walked up on a half-dressed Minta. Grabbing her by the waist and turning her back to his chest he whispered, "Do you have time to start a little party with me before the big party begins?"

George had always been a masterful lover, over the years he'd developed his skills into an art form and as he matured he'd become more deliberate in his bedroom exploits.

Pushing a hot-bodied George away, Minta scoffed, "Is that all you can think about George and especially at a time like this when something is going on with James and Scarlett."

Scratching the back of his neck and vexed due to his unmet needs George spoke with forced restraint, "How do you know something is wrong, darling?"

Playing the message on speaker, George listened to James' message he'd left for Minta.

"Now George you know it's not like them to miss a family function and couldn't you hear something in his voice that wasn't quite right? I'm going to call him back and find out why they aren't coming."

George knew Minta would not be satisfied until she called so any quality time he was looking to have with her before the party wasn't going to happen. With a heavy sigh, he zipped his pants up and thought to himself, "I'd like to know that for myself."

With a splash of cologne on to top of his outfit for the evening, George looked over at Minta and said, "I'm going downstairs, let me know what you find out."

Not even looking up, Minta nodded as she dialed James. No answer. She quickly dialed Scarlett. No answer. Minta dialed James again, this time the phone went straight to voicemail. The same happened when she dialed Scarlett's number, the phone went directly to her voicemail.

Their avoidance only fueled Minta. She sent both of them text messages:

"What's going on over there, call me back."

The doorbell rang, guests were starting to arrive but now none of that seemed to matter as Minta was concerned about why Scarlett and James decided against coming over.

Buttoning up her blouse, Minta thought, "*I'm going to go over there real quick and see what's up and I'll be back before the party starts. I may even bring Chandler back with me.*"

Checking her phone, there was still no reply back from James and Scarlett. Minta brushed up her hair and made her way downstairs. Seeing their family and friends arriving, she eased out of the back door and rushed through the neighborhood to James and Scarlett's house.

The ringing doorbell didn't register with anyone at the Hartgrove residence. James wasn't there and Scarlett and Chandler were sound asleep.

The silence at the door only added more anxiety for Minta as she began to think the worst. Her scattered thoughts were broken up when George's special ring tone blared out into the open air at James and Scarlett's front door."

"Minta, where are you? Did you forget we are having a party? People are asking about you and I go to check on you and you are gone and haven't even said a word to me. What's going on with you? Did you find out something about the kids? Answer me Minta."

"If you'd give me a chance I would answer you, I came down here to the kid's house to see what's really going on with them. Calm down, I'm on way back home. I'll be there in a few minutes George."

Minta hung up before George could respond.

"Is everything alright George?" Rena asked with Derrick standing behind her.

Not sure how to respond, George chuckled and said, "Hey y'all, hey listen, by chance have either of you heard from James or Scarlett today?"

Rena spoke up, "Um yeah, I got a text from James a while ago saying they were going to miss the party tonight. I asked him if everything was okay and he said something had come up but to give everyone their love. I didn't think any more of it, is something wrong?"

Waving his hand and trying to remain positive, George said, "I don't know of anything to be wrong but what's wrong right now is that we are having a good time at this party. C'mon let's go have a drink."

Just as they entered the kitchen, Minta walked inside and Travis came down the stairs. Everyone gathered around and yelled, "Happy Birthday Travis."

It was Travis' birthday, he was now fully accepted into the beloved Watson/Hartgrove clan and everyone was there to celebrate, well at least everyone.

With Marissa standing by his side, Cole offered up a birthday toast, "I love my sister, Lord knows I do but growing up, I always wanted a brother, someone to play and hang out with. While I didn't grow up with Travis, he and I have become close, he's the brother I always wanted and I'd like to wish him a happy birthday. I wish for nothing but the best for you in your life, I love you and happy birthday brother. Cheers."

Everyone raised their glasses in honor of Travis and the toasts continued around the room. With each kind word, Travis received them all with a wide grin that couldn't be contained.

As each person spoke, George stood tall with his chest out with a satisfied smile as he reminisced on the ups and downs they'd all experienced in getting to this very moment.

The room was filled with love and Minta cleared her throat to give a final toast, "Travis, Travis, Travis, oh Travis, boy have we come a long way in such a short period of time. Not long ago you showed up at a party and now we're having a party in your honor. As everyone here has said, you've shown yourself to be a true friend and member of the family.

I want you to know that I love you and I hope this is one of the best birthdays you've ever had. Happy birthday Travis."

Travis walked over to Minta and planted a kiss to her cheek and whispered, "Thanks Minta and I love you too."

Joining their embrace, George leaned in and said, "I think it's time to get this party started...turn up for what."

Cole spewed his drink across the counter as he laughed at his father, "Uh dad, I think you mean, turn down for what."

Waving his hands in the air, George replied, "I'm waving my hands in the air like and I'm waving them like I just don't care about whether it's turn up or turn down, can everybody say, oh yeah."

Everyone in the kitchen responded, "Oh yeah."

Travis' party had officially begun.

On one of her frequent trips to the bathroom, Marissa was in the guest bathroom when she heard the doorbell.

"Hi, can I help you?"

"Oh hi, I'm here to see Travis."

"Can I tell him who's here to see him?"

"No, it's a surprise. He'll know when he sees me. Are you going to invite me in?"

Taking time to think, Marissa glanced over the woman standing at the door with a suitcase in tow. Trying to stall as she felt uneasy about letting her into Minta's house, Marissa couldn't think quickly enough. Adding some distance between herself and the woman asking to come in, created an opening for the visitor to come in without permission.

Walking past Marissa, the intruder said, "Thanks for letting me in, now where's Travis?"

Following closely behind, Marissa shuffled in looking for Cole to explain.

Everyone had moved the party outside around the pool where George was grilling steaks and burgers.

Travis walked inside to grab a few drinks and heard, "Hey Travis baby...surprise. Happy Birthday."

Chapter 5

"Bishop...dad?"

Cayden-James flashed his flash light to illuminate his father's limp and un-postured body.

Wiping his face, Bishop smirked, "Wow, it's been years since you called me dad, hmmm, I must be in real bad shape."

Pulling out the chair next to Bishop, Cayden-James sat down, "Well, you are sitting outside in the pitch black dark."

The two Montgomery men both shared a laugh.

Taking a sip from his glass, Bishop asked, "I know why I'm out here, why are you out here?"

"Yeah man, you know, I come out here when I need to think."

"I know what you mean son, so do I. Even in the dark, it's so beautiful and peaceful out here."

The father and son were seated on a mound overlooking the Montgomery estate.

Extending his half-emptied glass, Bishop offered, "Have a drink with me."

Cayden-James' mouth flew open and in a high pitched voice he said, "Bishop?"

"What?" Bishop asked with a bark of laughter.

"Uh, I've never seen you take a drink a day in my life. Forgive me if I'm a little surprised by your offer."

Taking a slight pause before responding, Bishop turned to Cayden-James and asked, "By you seeing me drink this glass of wine, do you think it's going to cause you to stumble in your walk with God and be weakened in your faith[2]?"

Realizing most of the bottle was nearly gone and Bishop's willingness to share, Cayden-James figured, Bishop had become used to drinking. Shrugging off his concerns, Cayden-James replied, "Well of course not, I drink a glass or two myself every now and again. I was just surprised...shocked is more like it."

"I can understand your surprise son...seems like I keep getting surprise after surprise. Nothing in my life right now is predictable. Well, let me not say that, the only predictable thing in my life right now is I can depend on this bottle of wine to comfort me every night. You do realize this is Jesus approved right?"

Removing the glass and the bottle from Bishop's reach, Cayden-James poured himself a glass of wine.

"What are you even talking about, I feel like I'm talking to someone I've never met before," Cayden-James said with a chuckle.

"Oh you know, Jesus' first miracle was at that wedding where he turned water into wine, so yes, he's okay with me having a little sippy sip. In fact, I'm partaking in His blood, I'm only having a little communion."

Unsure of how to respond, Cayden-James just simply said, "Okay then."

Placing his now free hand on Cayden-James' shoulder, Bishop asked, "So talk to your old man, what's on your mind so that you needed to come out here?"

---

[2] **Romans 14:21**: *It is better not to eat meat or drink wine or do anything else if it might cause another believer to stumble.* (**NLT**)

Taking a sip from his glass, Cayden-James shook his head and steadied himself on the mound with a blush in his cheeks.

Bishop noticed and spoke before Cayden-James, "How's Ali, has she adjusted well? How's the project coming along?"

The flush in his cheeks deepened, smiling, Cayden-James said, "She's good."

"She's good huh and I guess I should be asking, how are you?"

Cayden-James laughed loudly, "I'm good Bishop and to answer to answer your question about the project that's one of the reasons I came out here to think."

"Uh-huh, one of the reasons....is Ali another one of the reasons?"

"Dude, what do you want me to say, do you want me to admit I can't stop thinking about her...because I can't. Bishop, there is something about her, she and I definitely have a connection but because I feel so guilty about what happened I don't know if I should try to pursue something with her."

It had been a long time since Bishop and Cayden-James had been in an exchange like the one they were in. They both were enjoying the time spent, yet all for different reasons.

Enjoying another sip from the glass, Cayden-James went on, "You know I invited her here to help create Trader Traits™ but in the meantime, I felt like there was something more I could be doing with my life and I started I guess what you would consider a prison ministry."

"Whoa, why am I just hearing about this C.J.?" Bishop asked. "This is wonderful news son, tell me more."

"You called me C.J., it's been a while since anyone has called me that." Cayden-James' tiger colored eyes fell soft and filled with an inner glow from the positive encouragement from his father.

"Well, the way I figured it, I was once in their shoes and I don't ever want to forget that. I was a prisoner like them, the only difference between me and most of the people incarcerated is means and opportunity. I've come to realize that a hustle is a hustle no matter how you look at it and most times people get locked up looking for a way to make it. I want to provide them with a better way to hustle."

Nodding his head in agreement, Bishop encouraged Cayden-James to continue on, hearing the growth and maturity in his youngest son caused him to pull in a deep breath and finish with a smile of satisfaction.

"What I'd like to do is begin working with inmates in prison but create a rehabilitation program, a pipeline where those interested in working with me will come out and learn how to invest money...the right way in an effort to provide for their families. Studies show high rates of recidivism because I think again, what is available for the person that just got out. Most people won't even hire convicted felons so they have no hope and nothing to look forward to on the outside to help further them in life. Unfortunately, wrong decisions, probably decisions made from trying to help the family cause them to go back to prison. I want to do something about that dad."

Scratching his scruffy salt and peppered beard, Bishop exclaimed loudly, "And I think you should, what's there to think to about. This sounds absolutely like a divine calling upon your life son, I think its's absolutely amazing and I support your 100 percent."

Standing up and looking out over the mound, Cayden-James clasped his hands together, "Thanks Bishop."

Interjecting, Bishop said, "No, no, no, call me dad...I like that. Yeah, call me dad, as a matter of fact, that's what I want you to call me from now on."

Raising his eyebrow, Cayden-James followed suit and said, "Okay, dad. Your support means a lot to me. The problem I'm having and the reason I came out here to think all boils down to Ali."

Swatting a bug from his foot, Bishop probed a bit, "Why is there a problem with her and what you are now trying to set up?"

"Well you know, remember when I came to you begging you to use your board seat to get her in school? I created the scholarship in honor of mother and then I invited her here under the pretense she'd work with me on the Trader Traits™ program while she worked to get her degree in Psychology." Hooking his thumbs into his belt loops, Cayden-James continued, "For all I've done to her family, I don't want her to think I lied and got her out here for no reason. I know I'll never be able to make up for what I did but I at least want to try. Dad, I really don't want to disappoint her."

Struggling to stand, Cayden-James extended his hand towards Bishop to help him up.

Placing his hand across his son's shoulders, Bishop began to admonish, "Son, in Proverbs, it says, in his heart a man plans his course but the Lord determines his steps. You know where I'm headed next right, the steps of a [good] man are directed and established by the Lord when he delights in his way [and He busies Himself with his every step] according to one of my favorite Psalms, Psalms 37:23." Cayden-James, it is a blessing of the Lord to be directed and He keeps the feet of those who follow His lead, I heard your heart in the plans you are considering and I believe you will be a blessing to a lot of people. Now, I know you don't want to disappoint Ali, there's a quick fix. However, I'm concerned about this connection you feel you have with her. How sure are you about that, I mean, you did just meet her, right?"

The thought of Ali caused Cayden-James to sit back down on the mound. He carried the weight of his guilt with him in his soul, she was the face to his past, to all of the people he'd hurt. Yet, he also believed she could be the face of his future.

With a deep sigh, Cayden-James responded, "I hear you dad and I do believe this new idea is divinely inspired, my issue, however is the timing of it. Do I go ahead and continue on with the project Ali is out here for or do I put that on hold to develop the other one? You've questioned me about the time frame in which I've known her. To that, all I can say is that when you know, you know. She reminds me so much of mother."

"Do you think that's the reason you are drawn to her, could you simply be missing your mother?"

"I hear what you're saying dad but it's more than that. Don't get me wrong, I miss mother so much, there isn't a day that goes by where I don't think of her. All I meant was she has a lot of the same qualities mother had and I like that...I really, really like that."

In a fatherly tone, Bishop responded warmly, "Talk to Ali. Let her know about the new project, be upfront and honest with her and see what she says. That'll be the easy part, I'm sure once you tell her the details; I think you'll be surprised at how she responds. Now, with respect to the developing feelings you have for her, the best advice I can give you is to one, take it slow and two, follow your heart."

Bishop's breath slowed with memories from the love of his life as he talked to Cayden-James about Ali. He mentally replayed past events from his life where he knew what the possibilities of love felt like. The freshness of a new relationship and the joys and comforts that one could provide was the cross roads Cayden-James now found himself and Bishop desired to go back and revisit those moments. Only he was now mourning the loss of his lady love. The question was, who was he actually mourning, Regina or Delores?

Before Cayden-James could respond, the grounds keeper, Charles rolled up in a golf cart beckoning the two Montgomery men, "Sir, we need you back up at the house."

Hurriedly, Bishop and Cayden-James jumped inside, throwing his hands up in the air and bracing himself, Bishop exclaimed, "Oh Lord, what now?"

Charles pounded his foot against the peddle of the golf cart and said, "Hold on guys, I'll explain on the way up."

Chapter 6

"Are you just going to stand there or are you going to greet me like you said you would when you saw me, baby?"

With a gaping mouth that opened and closed a few times without any sound, Travis was at a loss for words. His brain did finally kick in to reach out for Amira and kissed her on the cheek saying slowly, "Hi."

Leaning in closer to Travis and licking her lips, she whispered into his ear, "That's all you have for me, I was looking for a little more than that, aren't you happy to see me?"

Stepping back a little and squeezing Amira's hand, he said, "Of course I'm happy to see you...surprised but happy."

Wrapping her arms around Travis' waist and pulling him closer, Amira said, "Well, we'd been talking about when we were going to see each other again and I knew your birthday was coming up so I decided I would surprise you and..."

Speaking up and rubbing the back of his neck, Travis declared, "I'm definitely surprised."

Running her fingers across his face, Amira looked into Travis' face with a smile of seduction and said, "Mission accomplished."

Amira and Travis met while he was vacationing with the family on Chee Chee Island. They met his first night. Feeling nervous about being with the Hartgroves and the Watsons on a family vacation was somewhat overwhelming so he decided to go look for the spot where the locals hung out and there he met a striking Amira Rosier, a native Chee

Cheeian. For the rest of his time there they spent every night together until his accident. Travis and Amira had been communicating long distance since he returned back to Jordan.

By being prepared better what Travis actually meant and thought was, "*I just got into the good graces of my family, George hooked me up with a job at his old bank and I'm in school working on my degree and I don't need you popping up here where I live with, oh my God, Minta's house unannounced, I would have prepared better by getting you a hotel room, clear across town until I could introduce you.*"

Sticking her head through the door, Minta looked in and called out for Travis, "Hey birthday boy, I thought you were grabbing us something to drink, what's taking you so long, you need some help?"

Amira's eyes sparkled, oh wow, is that Minta? I've heard so much about her, I'm going to go meet her, c'mon introduce me to your family."

Hesitating, Travis tried to pull Amira back, "Wait a minute. What are you doing?"

Minta stepped inside the doorway and called out again, "Travis, honey, I said do you need some help?"

Breaking Travis' hold, Amira walked over, grabbed a few drinks, and marched over to Minta saying, "No, here we are and here are your drinks. Nice to meet you, I'm Amira."

Amira's eagerness caused Minta to pull back slightly, "Okay, Miss Amira. Nice to meet you and thanks for the drinks," as she flashed a glance and made eye contact with Travis who smiled nervously.

Turning around to Travis, Amira smiled and said, "Oh my Travis, she's more beautiful in person, now where's your dad, I think I met your brother's wife at the door, and oh yeah, is your sister here with her baby?"

Travis grabbed Amira's arm and drug her into the foyer away from everyone. Walking towards the door, he noticed a suitcase, thinking, *"Please Lord tell me that isn't hers."*

With crossed arms, Amira stood pouting while pounding the floor with her foot, "Why are you taking me away from the party, I came here to celebrate with you, I thought you'd be happy."

Travis's eyes squinted and he spoke without thinking, "I didn't invite you here."

Feeling rejected, Amira's hands fell down by her sides as the color drained from her face.

Pinching the bridge of his nose, Travis tried to explain, "What I mean is that, you coming here has taken me by complete surprise, you are moving way too fast. I'm still trying to process the fact you are here." Glancing over again at the suitcase, Travis said, "Speaking of, since you made these plans to come here on your own, where do you plan on staying and how long are you planning on being here?"

Amira stood back slightly with her hands cuffing the underside of her stomach saying, "I thought we'd stay with you."

With an increased difficulty in finding the right words, Travis began to feel his body temperature rise, "Uh come again. Who is we?"

Amira grabbed Travis' hand and placed it on her stomach and said, "Happy Birthday baby, surprise...I'm pregnant."

Travis' breath caught a hitch as he tried to speak, his skin tingled while his heart ramped up to full speed.

Stepping closer, Amira said, "Travis, baby, say something. Are you okay? I knew you would be surprised but all of the color in your face looks to be draining from your body, say something to me Travis."

In a suspended moment of time, Travis tuned out Amira's words and listened to the indistinct chatter and laughter from his party, those sounds were in direct conflict to the words coming out of Amira's mouth. The sounds from the party validated Travis as part of the family and having a life he'd only dreamed of. Those sounds signaled his acceptance.

Without saying a word, Travis picked up Amira's suitcase and grabbed her hand, leading her outside of the house.

Snatching her hand away, Amira yelled, "What are you doing? Are you trying to get rid of me Travis because I'm not going anywhere?"

"Calm down Amira and listen to me. You've been traveling trying to get here and this is not the time or the place to discuss...this issue."

Being confrontational, Amira snapped back, "This issue huh, you mean, our baby?"

Trying to keep his composure, Travis pulled out his keys and said, "We will talk about this later. Right now, I want you to take my car to this address and I'll meet you there later."

Despite living with Minta and George, Travis still had the apartment George rented for him.

Walking over to his car with Amira's suitcase, Travis placed her bag inside of the trunk and opened the door for Amira. "I'm texting you the address now, my apartment isn't far from here, text me when you get there. I will be there later."

With reluctance, Amira conceded, she was feeling tired and decided to go along with Travis' suggestion. Not to mention she could get settled in at his place.

With one hand to his forehead and the other to his hip, Travis stood and watched as Amira pulled off. Still in disbelief, he shook his head and turned to walk back inside to his birthday party. As he opened the door, he bumped into Stephanie. Upon seeing Travis, she smiled and said, "Hey you, where did you disappear to? Everyone's asking where the birthday boy is."

Travis' panicky laugh wasn't hard to ignore. Stephanie stepped back and asked, "Are you alright Travis?"

In an attempt to pull himself together, he said, "It was all an act baby, I came out here hoping you'd come look for me so I could do this." Leaning in and grabbing Stephanie by the waist, Travis lowered a sensual kiss onto Stephanie's lips.

Stephanie held onto Travis, welcoming more of his advances. She whispered, "I thought we were going to wait until later for this, what has gotten into you?"

Stephanie Sinclair, the daughter of friends to George and Minta. Dining out one night, George, Minta, and Travis ran into Stephanie and George picked up on how the light in Travis' eyes sparkled when he met Stephanie. In hopes of playing matchmaker again, since he'd been successful with Scarlett and James, he introduced Stephanie and Travis.

"You just look so good baby, you got all dressed up for me and my birthday; I couldn't take my eyes off of you and I couldn't take it any longer. I needed to get my hands on you, even if it is only for a few minutes."

"Slowdown playboy, we need to get back inside, you have a house filled with people here to celebrate with you for your birthday. You need to get back in there anyway and see what Minta and George are doing. You missed their dance off. Your dad's impersonation of bacon in the frying pan is hilarious."

Reaching for his hand, Travis placed his hand in Stephanie's hand and they walked back inside but not before she returned his advances with one of her own and whispered, "To be continued."

Chapter 7

"Hi Mom."

"Hey Ali baby, how's it going?"

"It's going okay, how are you?"

"Ali, I'm fine but I think you seem to forget I know you better than you know yourself and you don't sound like yourself. What's going on sweetheart?"

Biting the inside of her lip, Ali responded, "You know mom, I'm fine. Sometimes you just need to talk to your mama...you know what I mean?"

"I do. So what's on your mind? You keep telling me you are adjusting out there in California, is that not true? Has something happened?"

Inside the apartment rented by the Montgomery's, Ali sat Indian-style on her bed tapping her leg to settle her nerves.

"Everything is fine mom."

"Then what is it Ali?"

Inflating her lungs so she could release it all in one long sentence, Ali said as her breath flowed out of her, "I think I'm falling in love with Cayden-James and I'm not sure he feels the same way about me. Whew, there I said it."

In a light-hearted laugh, Ali's mother, Denise said, "Oh honey, you had me worried. This is easy stuff here. You're supposed to be out there getting an education but you are telling me you've gone out there and fallen for this guy?"

A flush crept over Ali's cheeks as she huffed, "I am getting an education mo-ther, a great one at that but there's something about this guy, I feel connected to him in a way unlike I've ever felt with anyone else."

Denise made a hmmm noise in her throat, her response was lackluster due to her mixed emotions. She voiced her conflict, "I hate to bring this up but have you forgotten what he did to your father?"

An intense thirst came over Ali, her dry mouth caused the next set of words to come out of her to be terse, "No, I haven't forgotten but it's not my job to constantly remind him of it either. Thank you very much."

Denise's eyes looked up towards heaven and she uttered a soft, "Thank you Lord." Pressing her hand against her heart, she said, "Well, I see you are willing to go to bat for him by being flippant with me. I'd been praying you would forgive him and it seems like you have and I'm grateful for that. Forgiveness is the greatest gift and if you think about it, forgiveness is essentially love so it is quite possible you do love him. Now, as your mom, I have to ask you this, do you feel like you're falling for him because he's doing all of these things for you? I don't want you to fall into that "White Knight" syndrome and I hope he doesn't have a savior complex."

Feeling a sudden lightness, Ali gushed, "I can see why you would ask that or have concerns but mom, he's absolutely amazing. In dealing with him, I can tell he made a mistake but he's paid for it. He's a kind spirit and he seems to be very deliberate about his life and how he treats people and I find that attractive. It doesn't help that he's quite handsome either."

Ali's giddiness was a clue to Denise that Cayden-James was someone special.

As only a mother could, Denise probed further, "So tell me, why do you think he's not interested or doesn't feel the same way?"

Ali loosened her legs and fell back on her bed, "Maybe because I can tell when a guy is interested and he doesn't seem to be. Sometimes when we are together, it feels awkward."

"Girl, that could be the sign right there that he's interested. He probably doesn't know how to approach you given the circumstances. You said it yourself how he's been through a lot, he simply may not be in the right frame of mind to let you know how he feels. Has that crossed your mind at all?"

Blowing air from her nostrils, Ali confessed, "No, I haven't thought about it like that. I just want him to tell me how he's madly in love with me and be done with it."

Denise laughed, "Um Ali, get your head out of the clouds sweetheart, it doesn't quite work like that. Listen to me, if it's meant to be, it'll happen. However, maybe you can test the waters by calling him and inviting him to hang out or you go to his house and take him some of those delicious brownies you make."

Snapping her fingers, Ali jumped up and said, "Hot dog, see, that's why I needed to call you. You always know the right things to say. I had forgotten all about my secret weapon brownies. He may not fall in love with me but he will fall in love with those. I'm going to take your advice and call him but first I need to go and make the brownies so I'll be ready to take them over later."

Denise smiled, "Okay baby, go ahead and let me know how everything turns out."

"I will, bye mom...and thanks, you're the best."

Chapter 8

Charles' golf cart ride seemed to be bumpier than usual. It could have been because of the news he was updating the Bishop and Cayden-James with.

Pulling up to the doorstep, Bishop walked in unsure as to what he was going to encounter.

Inside, Bishop saw Cherie slapping Mother Montgomery's hands away as she tried to comfort her in a corner. Yelling at the matriarch in the family, spittle flew across the room from her mouth. The intense gaze and reddening face was bothersome to Bishop and the scene was worse than Charles had described.

Bishop walked over shattered glass to get to Cherie. As he walked closer, a woman emerged from the guest bathroom, a woman with a familiar face but he couldn't place her.

"Excuse me but who are you and why are you here in my home?" Bishop asked.

Extending a handshake, Monica Stevens said, "Good evening Bishop Montgomery, I'm sorry to be here under such terrible circumstances but don't you remember, I'm part of Cherie's management team."

Shaking his head, Bishop offered, "Please forgive me, I didn't recognize you right away. So, you are who I have to thank for Cherie's outburst here?"

With a bowed head, Monica nodded and said, "Yes, unfortunately the rumors were indeed true, Johnson is dead. My partner is busy fielding phone calls and dealing with his family so I decided to come out and personally deliver the news to Cherie."

Touching her elbow, Bishop asked, "Would you excuse me for a moment?"

"Sure Bishop Montgomery, go right ahead."

Bishop stooped his enormous frame down to where Cherie sat with her arms folded around her legs rocking back and forth.

"Cherie."

Unresponsive, Cherie kept rocking.

"Cherie, c'mon let's get up. I need you to tell me what's going on."

Covering her ears with her hands, with tearful eyes, Cherie yelled out, "Leave me alone, get away from me right now." With a kicking motion towards Bishop Montgomery, Cherie declared, "I mean it...move."

Bishop Montgomery stood like an accordion with tense muscles as he cut his eyes towards Cherie and then his mother and son.

Motioning to his mother, Mother Montgomery followed her son into the kitchen.

Still in the corner, Cherie looked up at Monica who stood unbothered by Cherie's tantrums.

Cayden-James walked over to Cherie and said, "Get up."

Looking up at her cousin, Cherie said, "In case you didn't hear me, I want to be left alone."

"Oh, I heard you and I also saw you disrespect both my father and my grandmother now get your behind up." Cayden-James demanded.

Standing up to face her cousin, Cherie said, "Cayden-James, I'm going to tell you one more time to leave me alone before I really go off on you."

Cayden-James stood firm and said, "You won't be doing anything to me. In fact, I don't know if you realize it but you are standing up just like I told you to so who's doing what to who? Now, this is what I need to know. Why are you so worked up over this clown?"

Cherie shook her head in a way to indicate to Cayden-James she would not speak in front of Monica.

Glancing over his shoulder, Cayden-James turned and said, "Uh Monica, can I get you something to drink or is there something else we need to know concerning Cherie?"

Just as Monica was to answer, Cayden-James' phone rang. It was Ali.

Seeing Ali's number caused Cayden-James to smile but realizing he was in the middle of an intense situation cause his smile to waver. His lips pressed together in a slight grimace. He didn't answer.

Monica resumed her statement, "Uh, I think my work is done here for tonight. I'll be staying here in town for a few days so I'll be back to check on Cherie tomorrow. You guys take care."

Cayden-James walked Monica to the door and on his return, his phone rang again. Ali was calling again. This time, he answered.

"Hey Ali."

"Hey stranger. I haven't heard from you all day. How are you?"

Cherie stepped on a piece of broken glass, glass she'd shattered nonetheless and began screaming. In a broken dialogue, Cayden-James rushed Ali off the phone by saying, "Ali, this really isn't a good time. I have to go."

Staring at the phone, Ali's cheeks burned as she tossed the container of brownies in the trash.

Cherie's screams caused Bishop and Mother Montgomery to run out from the kitchen.

"What's going on now?" They both asked.

Mother Montgomery shuffled to get a first-aid kit to assist Cherie with her cut.

Cayden-James sat her down on the bottom step and said, "Start talking."

While in the kitchen, Mother Montgomery filled her son in on Cherie's extra-curricular activities and the video. She had not had a chance to tell him about Carson.

Cherie glared at her family and said, "Has anyone talked to Carson?"

Everyone responded, "No."

"I haven't spoken to Carson in a few days. Why do you ask?" Bishop inquired.

Cherie began to sob uncontrollably, "I asked Carson to go see Blue, Blue is now dead and no one has seen or heard from Carson."

Cayden-James scratched his head and said, "Do you seriously believe Carson had something to do with this? Why would you think like that? It's crazy to even suggest Carson had anything to do with some random drummer's death."

Cherie buried her face in her hands and then looked up and offered some perspective, "Is it so crazy to think that Blue was found dead covered in honey with nearly a million bee stings and not just any honey but Wilson's honey? And he wasn't just some random drummer, he was a celebrity drummer. Everybody wanted him to play for them."

Wilson's honey, an apiary steeped in tradition and Montgomery family history. Bishop Montgomery's great, great-grandmother belonged to the Wilson family and her parents were the owners of the thriving bee farm.

The possibility crossed everyone's mind but they all dismissed it.

Bishop was the first to object, "With everything Carson has going on, I don't see him involving himself to that degree. We all know Carson has done some messed up things in the past but none of that sounds like Carson."

Cayden-James then followed up behind his father, "Oh give me a break Cherie. Wilson's honey is a well-known brand; anyone could have used that honey. To me, that isn't enough to tie Carson to this guy's death. You are completely overreacting. I will say that whoever killed him like that has some real serious issues. That is some cray-cray stuff right there."

Mother Montgomery chimed in and said, "Carson is too self-absorbed to use honey on anything other than himself and his women. I can't see him taking the time to pour honey all over another man."

Bishop scoffed, "Mother."

Mother Montgomery cut her eyes at her son and said, "C.E. you know what I'm saying is the truth. Carson has a little freak in him, just like your father did and you probably do to," Mother Montgomery chuckled at her own words.

Bishop Montgomery failed to receive her style of humor, especially in such a sensitive moment.

Cherie dropped her hands between her legs as Mother Montgomery finished with her bandages and said, "But have y'all seen or heard from Carson? No. None of us have. By him being gone, he's going to look suspicious. I hate myself right now. Yep, I do. I got Carson involved and now look. I hope you all can see now why I'm so jacked up over this. What none of you know yet is when Monica first got here tonight she said Blue sent her a text that Carson was at his place and the next thing you know, Blue is dead. What if Carson was the last person to see Blue alive? Carson told me he was going to handle the situation for me. What if this was his way of handling it, huh? Hey, I know this sounds crazy. Trust me, I don't want to believe it either, I would never be able to live with myself if it is."

Mother Montgomery poked about a bit with Cherie, "Now Cherie, you told me other people were also in that video. Could it be someone else had a motive to keep the video from surfacing?"

Falling back onto the stairwell, Cherie belted out, "I don't know. He was blackmailing me because I was the only one with the amount of money he was asking for. It doesn't matter because if that video does get out, we all may get questioned."

Cayden-James stepped in, "Cherie, you say nothing about anything until we are able to find out more information. Do you understand?"

Impressed with Cayden-James' demeanor, Bishop agreed and reinforced his son's admonishment.

Mother Montgomery closed the box on the first-aid kit and said, "Lord, if Carson didn't kill the boy, who killed Blue?"

Cherie lifted her head to glance at her family and said, "All I know is, we need to find Carson and quick."

Chapter 9

"Godfrey."

When there was no answer, Rebekkah screeched his name again, "Godfrey."

This time, Godfrey came running. "What is it Rebekkah, are you okay?"

"I called you and you didn't come."

Sitting down on the bed next to Rebekkah, Godfrey said, "I was in the bathroom, I didn't hear you. Do you need something?"

Fluffing the pillows on her bed, Rebekkah made a demand, "I need you to go to the convenience store and get me an Icee...cherry and blue-raspberry mixed...extra-large."

Pulling the covers back to expose Rebekkah's feet for a foot massage, Godfrey said, "Rebekkah, you've had one every night this week, are you sure you need to have another one? That much sugar can't be good for the baby. Why don't I make you a fruit smoothie?"

Snatching her foot away, despite the glorious massage Godfrey was rendering, Rebekkah exploded, "Did I ask you for a smoothie? No, I didn't. You have no idea how intense these pregnancy cravings can be. When you want something, you want it. I asked you for an Icee and that's what I want. Now go get it and if you won't, I'll go and get it myself."

From the moment Carson kicked Rebekkah out, she was left with nowhere except back to Godfrey. With his incessant desire to nurture and love Rebekkah, he was glad things didn't work out with Carson and happy to have her back.

Only problem, Rebekkah was also relentless. Persistent in the fact she was carrying Carson's baby. Her never-ending conversations about the situation coupled with increasing hormonal fluctuations caused her emotions to be all over the place. She'd mastered going from calm to explosive in a matter of seconds.

Despite all of Godfrey's romantic gestures such as writing poetry for her, being supportive, encouraging her, giving compliments and expressing his love, she was obsessed with trying to prove Carson was the father of her unborn child.

Giving in, Godfrey got up, grabbed his keys and said, "I'll be back."

Rebekkah smirked and said, "I know you will."

When Rebekkah returned, Godfrey had a much different vision for how things would be. He felt like she was back where she belonged and they would finally be together like they'd planned years ago. They would raise the baby together because there was a possibility the baby could be his. Paternity wasn't an issue for Godfrey, he was happy to have Rebekkah back.

On the ride to the store, Godfrey let his thoughts get the best of him. *"I loved Rebekkah since the moment I laid eyes on her. She's mesmerizing in a sense most men do find it hard to resist her which is why I can't believe I let her go to him. I'm not sure why I let my disgust for Carson come in between us. I should have never agreed to her marrying him. Unfortunately, I let my hate for him rule over my love for her. She wasn't supposed to have feelings for him and she sure as hell wasn't supposed to get pregnant. We had a plan and she didn't stick with the script. I think Rebekkah saw a chance at the good life and must've tried to work it for all it was worth."*

Inside the store, Godfrey carefully made Rebekkah's drink according to her exact specifications. He'd learned his lesson. The first time he made it and it wasn't perfect, she poured the frozen confection in his lap. Any warm feelings he had for her in his tenderloins were now stiffened and not in a good way.

Nowadays, Godfrey walked around with a knotted belly, he barely slept and carried around a dullness in his chest, a feeling of heaviness.

Glancing at the clock in the store, Godfrey knew his time was limited. Rebekkah had him on a timer. When she needed her Icee fix, she needed him to not waste any time and get back with her craving.

Godfrey hurriedly paid for the drink and got back in the car where he was left with his thoughts again, "*I know I'm wrong for having her play the role to seduce Carson but part of me wonders why did she go along with it so easily? She declares she loves me as much as I love her but she seemed to jump at the chance without even thinking about it.*"

Pulling up in the driveway, Godfrey had a few minutes to spare before Rebekkah would be clocking for him. He allowed his head to fall back onto the headrest where he let his thoughts run freely. "*Rebekkah's pregnancy is starting to weigh on me. She's so different. She's moody all of the time and these crazy cravings are about to drive me insane. I need to figure out what my next step is. Carson divorced her without hesitation, he got out of that marriage quicker than he got in it so there's no reason she and I shouldn't go ahead and get married.*"

The silhouette of Rebekkah's body cast a shadow by the upstairs window. His minutes were up. He quickly jumped out of the car and ran inside.

Extending the Icee out to Rebekkah, he said, "Here you are my dear...just like you like it."

Delighting in the chilly treat, Rebekkah's snippy remark chilled Godfrey to his core, "It's about time," she said.

In a gentle tone, Godfrey offered an explanation, "There was traffic, night-time construction on the road."

In an effort to lighten the mood, Godfrey switched gears and made a suggestion, "How about we go away for the weekend? Let's get away, relax, have some fun, you know, before you can no longer travel. What do you think?"

Slurping up the last drop from her extra-large cup, in a now easy-going tone that contained a bit of wonder and surprise, Rebekkah asked, "Where would we go?"

Inching in closer to his beloved Rebekkah, Godfrey was enthusiastic for what was to come, happy she was even considering going.

"Well, you have two options, you can choose the location or you can let me surprise you, which would you prefer?" He asked.

Rebekkah's titled head and pursed lips was a good sign to Godfrey, he thought, "*I have her on the hook, she's thinking about it and hopefully this trip will get her mind off of pursuing another paternity test.*"

"Before I respond, I have a question. When would we leave because you know I'm trying to see about getting another paternity test done."

A firestorm was blazing inside Godfrey's head, he was shouting, yelling, ranting, and screaming all in his head,

"Jesus woman, are you kidding me? Get over the test already. Carson doesn't want to have anything to do with you, you'll never get close enough to him to get a DNA sample."

An impatient snort escaped from Godfrey, "We've been over this Rebekkah, how are you going to get another sample from Carson when he won't return any of your calls?"

Readjusting herself on the bed, she replied, "See that's the part I haven't figured out yet. He's not answering me and I rode by his house yesterday and it doesn't even look like he's living there anymore...it was weird. You know how sometimes you can tell a house doesn't have life in it or it seems abandoned? That's the feeling I got when I rode by. Nevertheless, I'm sure I have something of his that has is DNA on it, a trace of something that I can use. I just need to think real hard about it and figure out what that is."

"I don't want to wait too long Rebekkah. Depending on your answer, we could be gone in a few days. C'mon and let's go have a good time. All of this drama will still be here when we return."

Offering her commitment to Godfrey, Rebekkah spoke with a spark of hope, "Okay Godfrey, we can go and I'll even let you surprise me."

Typically, Rebekkah was one to always be in control and she knew she held the power to control Godfrey. Allowing him to plan the trip was her way of letting go and giving him room to lead.

Bumping shoulders, Godfrey could barely contain his excitement, he knew how big of a step this was for Rebekkah. He grabbed onto her arm and held onto it. He leaned in and kissed her. The kiss, it was sweet and tender. To him, it was a kiss of relief. To her, it was a kiss of submission. as sweet. To them both, the kiss was empowering.

Hating to break up their enchanted moment, Godfrey freed himself of Rebekkah and eased out of the bed, saying, "I'll be right back."

Unwilling to let him go, Rebekkah held onto him asking, "Why are you leaving me right now? I felt like we were kind of in the middle of something."

"We were and we will be in just a few minutes but I need to go downstairs to the kitchen. The way you kissed me I feel like I may need an energy boost for the rest of the night. I'm going to grab a little snack and I'll be right back. Can I bring you something back up?"

"Just make sure you bring yourself back up," she demanded as she demonstrated provocative moments meant to draw him in more, enticing him to hurry back up the stairs.

Rebekkah was an expert at controlling her partner's attention, she was masterful in her ability to put them under her spell.

Stumbling over his feet and words, Godfrey turned and said, "I'll be right back."

Downstairs, Godfrey reached for his phone and fired of a text message:

Godfrey: "**We need to talk**"
Karen: "**U ok...can u talk now**"
Godfrey: "**I'm good and no but 2moro**"
Karen: "**Fine, call me when u can**"
Godfrey: "**Gnite**"

Chapter 10

"What a wonderful party, did you enjoy yourself Travis?"

Overflowing with happiness and satisfaction, Travis was beamed as he looked around the room to who all was left, Minta and George, Cole and Marissa, Rena and Derrick and last but not least, Stephanie. With glances at each, he said, "Minta, I had the best time of my life. I have the best family and friends in the world."

Giving way a voice to the words he could never articulate growing up caused Travis to become somewhat emotional. He spoke with sincerity as he thought back over his life and even where he was two years prior and to see himself now surrounded by people who cared about him made it difficult for him to continue speaking. He pinched the bridge of his nose as if to stave off the ocean of tears that would have otherwise fallen.

Everyone in the group reached in for a group hug around Travis chiming in saying, "Ahhh. We love you Travis. Happy birthday Travis."

Shaking off the mushiness, George asked, "So where's the after party?"

Like clockwork, everyone cocked their heads toward George and voiced their shock, "George, are you kidding? What are you doing talking about after parties?"

In a dismissive wave of the hand, Minta answered on his behalf, "The only after party George will be attending will be the one he goes to in his sleep, in his dreams."

Marissa yawned while stretching, she stood to bid everyone good night, it had been a long day and she was tired.

Placing her hand on Travis' shoulder, she offered him one last birthday wish and waved goodbye to everyone. Cole followed her.

Rena and Derrick began to follow suit until George tagged Derrick to go out with him, "Hey Derrick, let's go out with Travis and keep the party going. Rena, you don't mind do you?"

Travis spoke up and said, "Rena might not mind but I'm not going with you guys George."

Laughing and playfully pushing Travis, George asked, "Why not son, it'll be fun."

Using his hands to show off Stephanie, Travis said, "Need I say more? My lady is here and I'd like to spend the rest of my birthday with her."

Crimson tones flushed through Stephanie's face.

Rena grabbed her purse and said, "Derrick, I'm going home. I'll see you guys later. Minta, are we still on for lunch tomorrow?"

"Yes, I'll stop by and pick you up," Minta offered.

George looked at Minta and said, "My son apparently has better plans tonight but my buddy, Derrick and I are going to go hang out for a while."

"Whatever George," Minta said wiping down the kitchen countertops before leaving Travis and Stephanie alone.

"It's just you and me kid. Are you ready to go birthday boy?"

"Oh yeah that's right, it's still my birthday for almost thirty minutes." Easing up to Stephanie, Travis whispered, "Do you have my present ready?"

"I sure do," she hinted.

"What is it?"

"Oh about that, it involves me wearing nothing but a bow."

Close enough to feel the warmth from each other's breath, Travis said, "That sounds like my kind of gift."

Stephanie responded, "Well then let's get ready to go. Since it's still your birthday, I'll drive you to your place. I'll be your personal chauffer."

Hearing the words, your place snapped Travis back into reality. His extended birthday plans were quickly interrupted with thoughts of...Amira.

Instantly, Travis felt feverish, his hands became slippery, his head started to pound and his stomach began to revolt.

He bent over to catch himself and rested his hands on his knees. The blood once flowing downwards switched and shot straight up in the opposite direction.

Stephanie pulled Travis against her shoulder, moving him to one of the bar stools. She held a narrowed focus on him, he was her sole area of concentration. "Travis, you are burning up. How did you get so sick so fast?"

Shaking his head, he couldn't quite possibly explain to her why his body was rebelling against him.

Making an unselfish gesture, Stephanie said, "I think we should postpone tonight and you should probably get some rest. Let whatever this is wear off, hopefully it is only one of those twenty-four hour bugs." Unasked, Stephanie left Travis' side to grab him a glass of water.

Travis heard what Stephanie said but thought, *"Or maybe this is an eighteen-year sentence."*

"I want you to go lie down and get some sleep. I'll call and check on you in the morning."

Taking a sip of water, Travis looked at Stephanie and said barely above a whisper, "I'm sorry Steph."

Addressing him in a positive way, Stephanie stroked Travis' forearm, "Oh nonsense, you have nothing to apologize for. Things happen."

Travis could feel Stephanie's sensitivity and her positivity yet he still offered her a sad smile.

"I'm going to go; I'll let myself out. Get some rest."

Stephanie and Travis' parting hug lasted longer than normal. He didn't want to let her go but he had to.

Seated at the kitchen counter, Travis pulled out his phone to see a number of missed calls and text messages from Amira.

He sent a reply text:

"I'm on my way"

Travis arranged for an Uber driver and walked outside to wait. As he got in the car, Minta saw him leave...without Stephanie.

Chapter 11

"So is this what our life has become? You staying out all night, me worried sick about where you are, who you are with, or what you're doing? You wouldn't answer any of my calls nor did you respond to any of my text messages. Where were you James?"

Completely removing his already loose necktie, James sneered and said, "Well good morning to you too Scarlett."

Blocking him from going anywhere else, Scarlett stood in front of her husband, her expanding belly separated them.

James braced himself and carefully picked Scarlett up and moved her out of his way. He walked in the bathroom and started the water.

Scarlett walked over to the bathroom and stood in the doorway with her arms and legs folded while she waited for him to finish his shower.

James emerged from the bathtub dripping wet. Scarlett had moved his towel; she'd draped it over her folded arms.

Seeing James in all of his glory took her to a place in her mind where she wished they could get back to. With baby Chandler becoming more aware to the world around him, James and Scarlett had become more creative about where their rendezvous took place in their house and the bathroom happened to be one of their favorite hideouts, the shower especially.

"Cute Scarlett. Real cute."

James walked past Scarlett without grabbing his towel. He plopped down on the bed without drying off, he decided he'd air dry.

"I'm exhausted." James announced.

Still with folded arms and now tapping feet, Scarlett shouted, "So are you just not going to tell me where you were or what you were doing? Are you not going to talk to me?"

"Scarlett, I'm not trying to get into anything with you right now. I'm tired. I'm choosing to not say much in hopes that I don't say the wrong thing. I did enough of that last night. Please, let me get some sleep and we'll talk."

Storming out of the room, Scarlett slammed the door behind her.

As she made her way downstairs, she heard the doorbell.

"Who is this at my house this early?"

Scarlett opened the door to find her mother, Minta on the other side.

Bulldozing her way into the house, Minta headed straight for the kitchen and went for it, "So you can't call your mother? You don't know how to return phone calls anymore. I'm glad I wasn't dying. I came over here last night and no one answered the door, where were you all? Tell me why I haven't heard from you when I know you know I've been trying to reach you. Why didn't you all come to Travis' birthday party?"

Scarlett's head began to swirl with all of Minta's questions.

"Good morning to you too mother."

"Oh, I thought I said good morning when I walked in. Good morning. Now, back to what I was saying, answer my questions girl. What happened to y'all?"

Since being served, Scarlett feared this very moment. She knew she wouldn't be able to keep the news from Minta but that didn't make having to tell her any less daunting.

Avoiding eye contact, Scarlett offered, "Coffee, tea?"

Intensifying her stare, Minta responded, "Answers. That's what I want."

Pouring a cup of tea, Scarlett said, "I wasn't feeling well and I told James I didn't feel like going."

"Are you feeling better today Scarlett?"

"Somewhat. I've had better days."

"Well, that explains you but that doesn't explain why James didn't come over and bring Chandler. You not coming shouldn't have kept them from coming over."

Scarlett knew Minta would continue until she found out the truth, Minta was like a yard dog searching for a bone. Scarlett faced the inevitable, she took in a deep breath and said, "Okay, here's the truth. Carson served with me papers yesterday. He's petitioning the courts for joint custody of Chandler."

Scarlett exhaled while Minta inhaled.

Minta exploded like a bad pressure cooker, "My grandson, my grandson, oh my precious grandson. That piece of, oh I can't stand Carson. I never could, I promise to God, I never liked that man." Pacing the floor, Minta was going from one thing to the next. Scarlett wondered how long it would take her to say those four magic words.

"Scarlett, I told you so. I told you not to trust that old snake in the grass Carson. I told you he wasn't to be trusted but no you for whatever reason, believed him."

Shrugging her shoulders, Scarlett thought, *"Well that didn't take long at all. She's managed to tell me how right she was and how wrong I was all the while making me feel worse than I already in less than five minutes. I think that might even be a new record for her."*

Minta's rant, caused the two males in the house to come down and check things out.

"Good morning Minta, I'm guessing she knows, huh?" James surmised.

Scarlett smirked and said, "How'd you guess?"

Minta took Chandler from James' arms and started in on him, "How could you let this happen, huh James? I guess the better question is, what are you going to do about it?"

James clenched his fist and said, "No hold on Minta. You are way out of line here."

Truth was, Minta was oftentimes out of line. She never really understood boundaries in most of her relationships. To her, there were no boundaries and especially when it came to her family.

Minta continued on as if James hadn't spoken. She continued to talk of Scarlett's bad judgement for telling Carson about Chandler.

James stopped her once again and said, "With all due respect Minta, I think you've said enough about my wife and the situation is being handled."

"In what way James, how are you handling this? What plans do you have?"

James walked over to Scarlett and held her hand, pulling her close to his side, "If you don't mind, I need to talk to my wife, all you need to know is that I have everything under control." Reaching for Chandler out of Minta's arms, James assured her, "We'll be in touch with you guys later."

Grabbing her things, Minta reached in and kissed baby Chandler and rubbed Scarlett across her back. "I guess I'll be leaving."

In muted tones, Scarlett said, "I'll call you later."

"Wow, is there no end to your mother? I mean, I love Minta and all but she can be a bit much. I understand this is a tough situation but good grief."

Scarlett giggled, "Dun dun dunnnnn, you've just experienced the wrath of Minta Watson."

James put Chandler in his high chair and pulled out a chair for his wife. "We need to talk."

"So you are ready to talk to me now?"

"Yes. So, I needed to get out of here last night. I needed to clear my head. I had all kinds of thoughts running through my mind and I didn't like where those thoughts were trying to take me."

"So where did you go?"

"California."

Scarlett's head flinched backwards, "Excuse me, come again."

"I called in a favor for the jet and I went out to pay Carson a visit, man to man."

Scarlett's mouth opened but it closed without anything coming out of it. Her mouth opened again but nothing came out. She tried once more and said, "What happened?"

"Nothing happened. He wasn't home. In fact, it doesn't look like he's been there for a while. I waited for a couple of hours but there was no activity in or out of that house. I purchased a burner phone while I was out there and dialed his number and it says the number is no longer in service."

Scarlett's thoughts were scrambled as she tried to understand and make sense of what James was saying. Where was Carson and why would he have her served only to disappear?

"This doesn't make sense to me honey." Scarlett confessed.

"I know which is why, I consulted with several lawyers while I was gone. I know I did everything by the book with Chandler's adoption but I wanted to make sure we had an iron-clad adoption agreement. I'm not sure what this clown's motives are but he doesn't have a leg to stand on. I don't know what he has going on and I really don't care but what I do know is I'm not going to let him come in and try to destroy my family. I was out all night making sure we are protected."

Kneeling down by Scarlett, James placed his head in her lap and wrapped his arms around her. "I love you and I'm sorry for how I responded to you last night. I was hurt. I was angry. I felt threatened and I lashed out at the wrong person, I took my frustrations out on you and I'm sorry." Lifting his head, he saw streaming tears fall from Scarlett's face. She ran her hands down his unshaven beard. James' voice wavered as he asked, "Will you please forgive me?"

Scarlett pulled James up to her, "Of course I forgive you and I ask for your forgiveness as well. I'm sorry honey."

James and Scarlett made up while Chandler dropped his food on the floor and laughed while doing it.

Together, James and Scarlett cleaned up the mess and Chandler who squealed and laughed every time they wiped his face.

His giggles were precious, he was innocent and ignorant to the war surrounding him.

His mother picked him up and held him close wondering, *"Where is your father and why is he doing this to us?"*

Chapter 12

"Wake up. I said wake up."

Shoving a sleeping Travis, Amira continued to pester.

The morning sunlight peered through Travis' bedroom window, the glare was more uncomfortable than Amira's poking and prodding.

Raising his elbow to guard against Amira's jabs, Travis spoke up, "Stop it. I'm woke, can you give me a minute?"

Deepening her tone, Amira blasted Travis, "The way I see it, I've already given you plenty of minutes. Might I remind you how you shipped me off from your party last night, you got here late, then you crashed when you got here. The way you were snoring looks like I missed a grand old time at your birthday party. I want to know, when are planning to talk to me? I came all this way to see you and this is how you treat me?"

"Amira, you showed up last night at my family's house unannounced. Do you see how that might catch me off guard?"

Nodding, Amira said, "Yes, I could see that but you and I talked about me coming to see you. So, I didn't think it would be that big of a deal."

"No big deal? We talked about that a while ago. You and I haven't spoken in a few weeks. How I remember it, we did a video chat one day and then you like fell off the face of the earth. I called, I sent texts, I emailed you and nothing, you stopped responded."

Edging over closer, Amira tried to explain, "I had just found out I was pregnant and I was sick, I mean really sick. I could barely keep anything down and I needed to find out what was going on. I'm sorry I stopped responding, I was quite overwhelmed."

Inching away, Travis said, "Listen, I can understand being overwhelmed, I'm feeling it a bit myself. In fact, I'm going to need some time processing this. You want me to talk to you but I honestly don't know what to say to you. I'm still trying to wrap my mind around the fact you flew here, let alone you telling me you're having my baby."

Saying the words aloud caused Travis to shiver.

"I'm going to get up and get dressed because I need to get going."

"And where do you think you're going?"

"Not that I need to answer to you Amira but I'm going home."

"I thought this was your home?"

"It is but right now, my home is where my family is. That's where I've been staying lately and I need to head that way. I came here to check on you which I will continue to do but until I can make sense of this...I'm out."

Walking into his bathroom, Amira yelled out, "I can't believe you Travis. So, you're just going to leave?"

Before he shut the door Travis threw his hands up in the air and reminded Amira, "I think you keep forgetting, I didn't invite you here. I'm not doing anything to you; I'm trying to understand what's going on here and you need to respect that. Yes, you and I had sex...while I was on vacation, nonetheless and yes, we continued to talk once I returned but you stopped talking to me." Travis turned and marched in the bathroom to shower.

Fuming on the bed, Amira searched through Travis' pockets and found his phone. She thumbed through as much as she could before he reentered his bedroom.

The shower was good for Travis because he came out and said, "I can go and grab us some breakfast before I leave if you like. By you being pregnant and all, I guess it's important for you to eat right, huh?"

"Yes, that is correct and I am getting rather hungry."

Buttoning up his shirt, Travis gave a weak smile and said, "Well alright, I'll be right back."

In the short time Travis was gone, Amira quickly cleaned herself up as well. In a matter of minutes, she was showered, dressed, and in full makeup.

Evaluating Amira's appearance, Travis scoffed, "You did that quick. Going somewhere?"

"No silly. Where would I even go? I wanted to look nice for you when you got back."

Sitting down together made Amira smile. She placed her hand on top of Travis' and said, "This reminds me of the early morning breakfasts we had on Chee Chee Island. Do you remember?"

A thought flashed through Travis' mind, "*I would rather forget.*"

He swallowed the last piece of his bagel and said, "Yes, I remember."

Travis poured two glasses of juice, passing Amira her glass, he questioned her, "So you just up and left to come here, what did your family have to say about that?"

Amira exercised a long pause before answering, she took a sip of her orange juice and said, "They were fine. I'm a grown woman and I make my own decisions. The way I see it, they can either support me or not, either way, I do what I want."

Rinsing out his glass, Travis heard a knock at the door.

A thumping heartbeat signaled to Travis he was wary of who could be at his door. Had Stephanie realized he wasn't at the Watsons and decided to come over and check on him? If that were the case, that could be bad for Travis.

"Aren't you going to answer the door?" Amira asked.

Tapping his fingers against the countertop he said, "I hadn't planned on it. No one called to tell me they were coming over and I don't answer doors to unwelcomed guests."

Amira received the impact of Travis' backhanded comment.

The knock continued.

Amira stood and said, "Well if you won't, I will."

Travis intercepted her before she got to the door.

Taking in a deep breath before looking through the peep hole. He gasped at who he saw.

Opening the door, he said, "Minta? What are you doing here?"

Still on level one hundred, Minta charged inside saying, Minta said, "Travis, are you hung over or something? You sent me a text saying you needed me to come over here as soon as I could. I was leaving Scarlett's house so I came on over. What's up?"

Travis' body froze.

"Speak up boy, I don't have all day. What do you need, why did you call me over here?" Minta inquired.

Scratching the back of his neck, Travis confessed, "Minta, I'm sorry but I didn't text you."

Throwing her hands down, Minta shook her head saying, "This doesn't make any sense." Pulling out her phone, she said, "This is your number. So if you didn't text me, who did?"

Before he could respond, Amira emerged from the kitchen and declared, "I did."

Travis' eyes widened.

"You did what?" He exclaimed.

Minta sized Amira up from head to toe. She stepped closer to her and said, "And who are you?"

Speaking in a bubbly tone, "I'm Amira, remember? We met last night."

With a slight nod and a flat tone of voice, Minta said, "Uh-huh. So tell me, why are you playing childish games by sending text messages to me from my son's phone?"

Travis nearly fainted.

Hearing Minta refer to him as a son was more than he could handle. He didn't want her to know about the mess he was in, he didn't want to disappoint her and especially after hearing her acceptance of him.

"Maybe we should all sit down," Amira suggested.

"No thank-you, I think I'll remain standing." Minta replied.

Speaking through his clinched teeth, Travis asked again, "Why did you text her Amira?"

Amira crossed her hands and folded them in her lap, "You said you needed help sorting things out and I know how you've said Minta is great at creating win-wins for people so I thought she could help."

Keeping an eye on Amira, Minta glanced at Travis who was drenched in sweat. "Travis, what is she talking about?" Minta asked.

Travis grabbed Minta's hand and started moving towards the door, "Minta, do you mind if I speak with you outside?"

Amira sat back on the sofa with a supreme look of confidence and satisfaction in herself as the door slammed shut.

"What's going on Travis? I saw you with that woman last night and when I walked in the kitchen, you looked like you'd seen a ghost. Why is she playing these silly little games, trying to trick me into coming over?"

Clasping his hands together, Travis admitted, "Minta, I really don't know where to begin or how to even tell you this."

With a blank expression, Minta offered, "Try me."

Travis rubbed his forehead and pinched his eyes shut.

"It's complicated. I don't want to bother you with this."

"I'm already in it. Talk before I go and ask Miss Amira." Minta demanded.

Travis explained the situation to his stepmother.

Truth be told, he felt better. Relieved in fact.

Jingling her keys from her purse, Minta's response was direct, "Meet me at the house later for dinner. Don't leave anything here you don't want her to have access to."

"Yes ma'am."

Inside the apartment Amira asked, "Where's Minta? Is she not coming in to talk with us?"

"No Amira and I don't blame her. Why did you pull a stunt like that? Listen, I've been trying to be patient and understanding with but this is getting old, quick."

Reading Travis like a book, Amira said, "Are you as patient and understanding with Stephanie?"

"That's it; I've had enough." Travis went from calm to explosive in no time flat. He grabbed Amira by the arm, inflicting more pain on her than he realized, he was unaware of his own strength. Despite the pain, she smiled at him and said, "I must be hit a nerve."

Travis released her arm and said, "Um, it's best I leave. I'm taking my car back. I'll have some food delivered here and I'll check on you later."

With the door closing behind him, as if she was singing in a chorus, Amira said, "Whatever Travis. Don't be gone too long, who knows what I might find to do around here."

Chapter 13

"Hey, I'm glad you could meet me so early."

"Well, you didn't leave me with much choice. You had me worried with that cryptic message you sent me last night."

Godfrey handed his cousin a cup of coffee, "I brought your favorite."

"You're bringing me my favorite coffee; this must be serious. Lay it on me, what's going on Godfrey?"

Laughing, Godfrey said, "I can't just be a nice guy and bring you some coffee? You feel like I have some ulterior motives here or something?"

"Well don't you? Seriously and all jokes aside, what do you want?"

Godfrey let out a small sigh, "Do you remember those DNA tests you ran? Do you still have the results?"

"I knew it. I knew you weren't just being a nice guy. Tell me, oh please tell me Godfrey, why would I still have the results to tests you told me to destroy?"

Throwing his head back with his eyes closed, Godfrey whispered, "It was worth a try." Repositioning himself on the park bench, Godfrey said, Karen, I know I asked you to destroy the results, I just needed to check with you, maybe sometimes you all have backups or something."

Karen and Godfrey were cousins. Distant cousins but cousins still the same. When Rebekkah left Carson, he needed a nurse. Unbeknownst to Carson, Godfrey arranged for his cousin, Karen to become Carson's caregiver. Inside the home, Karen was available to report on everything Carson did and especially after he mistakenly shot Rebekkah. She was Godfrey's eyes and ears.

Tilting her head, she asked, "Do you realize I could lose my job if my agency found out about what I did for you? Luckily, I was more than careful, nothing is traceable back to me. Look here, I tested both your DNA and Carson's against Rebekkah's baby. You said, you weren't interested in the results, you only wanted it to look like Carson was not the father and so that's what I did. I don't know who that baby is, for all I know, it could be the mailman."

Expressing his gratitude, Godfrey said, "I know, I know and I owe you big time. Please don't say the mailman."

Changing the subject, Karen said, "Dude, what's going on with you? You weren't raised like this. What is this obsession you have with Carson? I mean, spying on him and gathering information on him over the years, what gives? Now that I think about it, your all-out campaign to sabotage him is quite frankly, petty and beneath you. You pawned off the girl you claim to love off on him and now she's pregnant and has no clue who the father of her child is. Does that not do something to you on the inside?"

Karen's words stung. Oftentimes the truth does hurt.

She continued, "Man, you were born and raised in the church so I don't have to tell you how wrong this is. I've accepted the responsibility for the role I played but Godfrey, you need to deal with this. You say you love Rebekkah, then stop hurting her. I think you're hurting rather than helping her."

A few early morning joggers ran past them as they sat in their childhood park.

In a brief moment, Godfrey allowed himself to feel the burden of his obsessive nature. His determination to hurt Carson drove him to these extremes Karen was referring to and for what. The moment was short-lived because the pain was too strong for Carson to endure. He couldn't sit in his truth and the possible irreparable damage he'd caused.

Godfrey sat with an unnatural stillness, not meeting Karen's gaze.

Rubbing her hands across his shoulders, Karen said, "I wasn't trying to be Debbie Downer but I think you need to consider what's really at stake here. Most times, situations like this don't work out well. However, for your sake, I hope this works out the way you want it to."

Godfrey cleared his throat and thanked Karen for coming to meet him.

"I'm going to get ready to go, I have a night shift assignment tonight."

Godfrey stood to hug Karen, "Hey, before you go. Have you seen Carson lately? Are you still working for him?"

Karen let her shoulders down, "After all that I just said, you still have the nerve to ask me about him? You are worse off than I realized."

Godfrey chuckled, "No, no, no it's not like that. Trust me, I heard what you said. I was only asking because Rebekkah has been trying to reach him and he hasn't returned any of her calls and she said she rode by his house and it looks empty. She's trying to get another test done."

Shaking her head, Karen said, "Good luck with her getting another test out of him, he was so mad when he got those results. But to answer your question, he cancelled my assignment a week and a half ago. He paid me a bonus and didn't give a reason for the termination, the agency alerted me saying the assignment was over."

"Hmmm, interesting. Okay Karen, well, I'll be in touch. Thanks again for everything."

Chapter 14

"Knock, knock, have time for a visitor?"

Glancing up from his desk, Bishop said, "Dottie? What are you doing here?"

Not waiting on an invitation to enter, Dottie stepped over the threshold to Bishop's office. "You seemed a little distracted last night so I thought I'd stop by."

Nowadays, despite Bishop being on hiatus, he still worked behind the scenes of Wondrous Works as he made room for his brother, Claude to lead the church.

"You didn't have to do that."

Grinning, Dottie replied, "I know I didn't have to but I wanted to."

Initially, Bishop was grateful for Dottie's kindness but now she was becoming more of a drain to him, he was becoming annoyed but he wasn't sure how to tell her without coming off as a jerk.

Walking closer, Dottie plopped down a picnic basket and said, "I tried calling you and you didn't answer. You said you weren't sure if you'd stop by for dinner later so I wanted to check on you and also bring you this."

Bishop's voice, strained and tense, "Dottie, now really isn't a good time. I'm swamped and I don't mean to be rude but I have several things going on at once that need my attention." Having a quick look, Bishop pointed towards the basket and said, "What's this?"

Releasing an appreciative sigh, Dottie smiled and said, "I brought you some lunch."

Continuing with his work, Bishop explained, "Dottie, this is too much. Really now, You've already done enough. I appreciate the gesture but I need to get back to work."

Dottie enjoyed being in Bishop's presence and her intrusion upon his time didn't register as such with her, it filled a need she had within to be supportive and a source of encouragement, it made her feel important. In turn, maybe he'd see how happy he was with her.

Peering over his desk she countered, "You have to eat don't you? Surely you can take a few moments to grab a bite to eat. C'mon, I'll even set it up, it won't take long, I promise."

Walking outside of Bishop's office, Dottie laid out her spread. Bishop's intimate private sitting area transitioned well between the indoor beautiful décor inside his office to that of the luxurious outdoor oasis. He would oftentimes retreat out there to recharge and regroup. He would sit out there and allow himself a moment to relax and think on the goodness of Jesus. He could go out there and escape from it all, it was sacred and consecrated ground.

Moving toward the exit, Bishop glanced at his watch and hinted again about him being busy.

"If you are as busy as you say you are, you are going to need to keep your energy up and the only way to do that is eat, so come on and sit down." Dottie declared.

Sitting down opposite of Dottie in his favorite cushy chair, Bishop grabbed his plate, stuffing his mouth with a fork full. There was no doubt about it, Dottie's food was good.

Bishop Montgomery loved eating outside, he loved taking in the fresh air and enjoying the beauty of the woodlands and dark vegetation of his beloved Wine Country. The views were often picturesque and Bishop oftentimes joked around saying God must be an artist.

The only sounds heard was of Bishop chomping, few words had been spoken between the two. Dottie decided to change that, she broached a decision she was facing. "Do you mind if I ask your opinion on something?"

Still not talking, Bishop nodded his head as he continued to scarf his lunch down.

Dottie rose up and said, "So, I've been offered an opportunity to go start and partner with another Bed and Breakfast in Michigan. Apparently Michigan is experiencing a boom in local tourism from their wineries and a developer contacted me about going and doing some business there. I've been in talks with them for weeks and everything seems to check out, I just don't know if I should go. I haven't spoken to Delores about it yet, I mean, I'm not sure how long she plans to stay here and if I left, I don't know who would run our inn?"

Dottie knew it was a shot in the dark, yet she took her chances. She was hoping and praying Bishop would ask her to stay, she sat still, jumping up and down in the inside, as she listened for his response.

Taking a big gulp, Bishop said, "Dottie, it sounds like an awesome opportunity; I think you should do what works for you."

Dottie's face went slack, she said, "I guess you're right; I do need to do what works for me." Clearing Bishop's plate, she offered, "Would you like something to drink?"

"Yes, I'll take whatever you have and then I must get going."

"Sure thing."

Finishing up Dottie's infamous lemonade, Bishop made a move to get up.

Dottie asked him one more question, "Why did you choose her over me?"

Before he could answer, Bishop Montgomery was knocked out.

"Man, that stuff worked quicker than I thought, let me hurry up," Dottie said to herself.

Carefully situating Bishop the way she wanted him, props and all, sunglasses to cover his eyes and sunglasses for herself. Dottie grabbed her selfie stick and posed with Bishop Montgomery as if they were having a romantic lunch with the hills of the vineyards as their backdrop.

"I'll snap several pictures to get the best one," she thought.

Once her little photoshoot was over, Dottie cleared up everything. She removed any evidence of her being there. Leaving Bishop out in the elements of the noon day sun, Dottie made a beeline for the door.

Within minutes, Mother Montgomery walked into her son's office. She was there to discuss Cherie and Carson in further detail and what was going to be their plan of action. Mother Montgomery found Bishop sprawled out in his chair, his favorite chair. She pushed on him, he didn't move. She called for him to wake up, he didn't answer. She checked his pulse, he had a strong one. Mother said a quick prayer in her heart.

As she was about to call for help, she noticed a pair of sunglasses, female sunglasses and called the head of security, Jason, instead.

"Hey baby, this is Mother Montgomery, can you tell me if my son has had any visitors today?"

"Hello there Mother, um let me check for you. It looks like a Dottie Bolton was here and she just signed out actually. Baby, I need you to do two things for me, get me the video footage of my son's office in the last hour and bring it to me and is the nurse here today?"

"Yes ma'am."

"Have her come to Bishop's office right away, can you do that for me baby?"

"Anything for you Mother Montgomery, give me a few minutes."

Jason entered the office after the nurse. The ministry's nurse was attending to Bishop while Jason reviewed the footage with Mother Montgomery. He fast-forwarded the film until he saw Dottie enter the office. From there, he and Mother Montgomery watched as if they were at a feature film at the movies.

With his hand over his mouth, Jason asked, "What do you want me to do ma'am?"

The smelling salts worked on Bishop, he was awake yet groggy while the nurse checked his vitals.

Mother Montgomery rose up from Bishop's desk and walked outside towards her son. The nurse gave a nod of approval that he was fine. "Son, how are you feeling? Do you know why you may have passed out?"

Rubbing his forehead, Bishop said, "Not really mother. Everything feels a little hazy right now but I feel fine. I guess I'm more stressed out than I realize."

"Alright son, as long as you are okay. I came to talk to you but I need to head out for a while. I'll be back."

Walking back inside, Jason asked again, "What would you like for me to do about this ma'am?"

"Nothing...dumb broad, did she forget this place is under video surveillance? I don't want you to do anything, I'm going to handle this one myself. I do need you to get me that video though."

"Oh yes ma'am, here, let me hold your phone. I'll put it on there and let me show you how to access it when you need it."

"Thank you baby. Mother Montgomery is going to get out of here now. I'll be seeing you."

Chapter 15

"So, how'd it go last night with Cayden-James?"

"Mom, there are other things I'd rather talk about, can we talk about those?"

No, we can't. You called me last night wanting advice, all starry-eyed, and sitting on cloud nine about this guy and now I want to know what happened. Did you bake the brownies like I told you?"

Accusing her mother, Ali lashed out, "How could you tell me to bake him brownies?" That was the worse advice you could give."

Ali's mother repeated back what was said to her, "How could I tell you to bake him brownies? You agreed the brownies were a great idea. What are you talking about girl?"

Ali ran her hands through her hair, "He never got the brownies," she exclaimed.

"I don't know what's going on with you, girlfriend but you better switch gears in how you are speaking to me," Denise scolded.

Ali filled her mother in on her phone exchange with Cayden-James the night before.

Denise cleared her throat, "That's all you had to say instead of getting all huffy-puffy with me. Well, have you heard from him today?"

"Nope."

"I hope you are kidding about tossing those brownies, you are kidding right?"

"Nope."

"Ali," Denise yelled.

Ali burst out laughing at her mother, she knew how much her mother loved those brownies so to hear her scream over them being thrown away made her laugh.

Denise cracked up as well.

Ali's laugh was cut short when she roared, "Argh."

"What is it Ali?"

Ali scoffed, "Speak of the devil and he shall appear. Cayden-James is calling me."

"Go, answer him."

"Nope."

"Ali, stop it with the nope(s), seriously. Answer that boy, he may be calling to apologize or make up for last night."

"Oh, I hate you sometimes...hold on."

Denise raised Ali in a more unconventional way, growing up, she didn't make Ali call her mom, she was fine with her calling her Denise. She raised her more as a friend than a daughter. Denise allowed Ali to express herself without many limitations, she rarely told her no.

The interesting thing about their relationship was now that Ali was an adult, they assumed more of a mother/daughter relationship.

"Hello."

"Hey Ali, are you busy?"

In short and direct responses, Ali said, "I'm talking to my mom. What's up?"

"Oh nothing, I just wanted to check in today and say sorry for last night. Things were crazy and I probably shouldn't have answered but I saw where you called back to back so I thought something was wrong. I hope I didn't sound too short with you; I was just stressed out."

Softening up, Ali said, "Oh, it's okay...I understand."

Even though she said she did, she really didn't. She couldn't understand why was his family always having some type of crisis going on.

"I know you're talking to your mom so I'm not going to keep you, you want to grab a pizza later?"

Biting her bottom lip, Ali was slow to respond but she did finally, "Yeah, that sounds cool. I'll text you later."

"Mom, you still there?"

"Yes, I'm here. That took a minute, apparently you didn't hang up on him. What did he want?"

"You were right, he apologized. He wants to go out for pizza later."

Denise beamed, "Bingo. I have a sixth sense about these things baby girl, so let's rewind. You were kidding about those brownies; you still have them don't you because you need to make sure he gets them tonight."

"Nope."

Denise threw up her hands in the air, "For the love of God and all things holy, what is wrong with my child?"

The two women shared a laugh.

"Well, I guess you need to hang up with me and get to baking...again. And listen, if something happens tonight and for whatever reason you don't get to see him, please don't throw away another batch of brownies, just put them in the mail tomorrow for me."

Ali laughed and assured Denise, "Okay mom, I will."

Chapter 16

"Rena, I'm sorry I had to cancel lunch earlier but honey when I tell you all of what I've been through today, you'll see why and figure out why I'm having a family dinner this evening."

Rena stood at Minta's rinsing sink, washing off dirty carrots, freshly picked from Minta's garden.

The two had become fast friends, they were both enjoying their retirement and spoiling Chandler. Rena had even begun attending church with Minta and the rest of the family. With both of their children being married they had become a collective source of support for the young couple.

Minutes later, their pride and joy walked through the door with his mother, Scarlett waddled her way into the kitchen with her son on her hip.

Both women, Rena and Minta kissed him on his cheeks.

Minta looked at her daughter and said, "The way you are moving, I know you haven't been doing much walking and talking, have you?"

Rena dried her hands and relieved Scarlett of Chandler who was appreciative.

She sat down with a big sigh, "I sure have not. You know that campaign has taken a life of its own, I really don't have much to do with it anymore. James' company runs it and I probably won't be doing any real walking and talking until after I have this baby. Thank you Rena, that boy is getting so heavy, he is growing like bad weeds."

Rena smiled and said, "Yes he sure is, he's getting out of the way for his little sister." With a quick rub to Scarlett's belly, Rena put Chandler in his high-chair to feed him.

"We don't know if it's a girl or a boy. You know we are waiting to find out."

Rena winked and said, "You may not know but I know."

Scarlett scouted the kitchen for something to eat and said, "What is so important that I had to cut my shopping trip short and cancel my dinner plans with my husband? Can you please tell me why I'm here and where is everybody else?"

Minta went down the list, "Well, Cole and Marissa were going to leave today but she's not feeling well, she said she feels achy, almost like the flu, and based on today's events, I asked them to stay over another night. She's upstairs resting and Cole is out getting some things I forgot at the store. Derrick and George are playing golf. Travis should be here soon and hopefully James will be here soon. He said, he'd be here shortly after work."

"Okay, thanks for the roll call but what is this 'lil family dinner all about? Wasn't everybody here last night?"

Scarlett was thinking Minta was going to make a big deal about the custody petition so she wasn't thrilled about being there but when Minta comes calling, you best answer.

Minta continued to busy herself with the dinner preparations not even responding to Scarlett.

The next to arrive was James. "Hello everybody," James said as he greeted all of the gorgeous women in his life.

He kissed Chandler on his head and smiled at Scarlett who was excited to see him. She stood up and grabbed a bag she'd left by the door and asked him to follow her out by the pool.

James sat down and Scarlett placed a beautifully wrapped box in his lap.

Shaking the box, James said, "Wait a minute, it's not my birthday and it's not Christmas, what's going on here?"

Scarlett stood and rubbed her belly, she was pleased to see her husband smiling and cheerful, a stark contrast to his behavior twenty-four prior.

Inside the box was a pair of simple, yet elegant, chestnut colored lace-up oxfords to replace the shoes he'd lost the night before. The card read:

"I've always been told women shouldn't buy men shoes because they'll walk away from them in them. However, I'd like to offer a different perspective. Let's use these shoes as a symbol that we will always walk, side by side, hand in hand, together and for always.

- Your wife, Scarlett."

James stood up and joined Scarlett saying, "I love the gift and I love you. By now, you should already know this but I will never walk away from you; I'm here for the long haul, sweetie. We have children to raise together and I want to be the man who will love you the way you deserve. I'm here with you, hand in hand...forever."

The setting sun's afterglow covered them as their heads instinctively tilted to receive each other's lips. Scarlett threw her arms around James as he reached down to caress her growing body. She realized James still hadn't shaved and his sexy stubble was forming a near perfect five o'clock shadow. The new look added an edge to him, in a way, Scarlett began to swoon for James all over again. When their lips did meet, they melded together with a renewed sense of respect and dedication for one another.

And just like that, their moment of reconciliation was interrupted, Minta was yelling from the French doors, "Everyone's here, come on inside."

Minta corralled everyone together in the kitchen, she ordered everyone to get some food and then she'd explain why she'd called the family meeting.

Everyone grabbed a plate, except Marissa.

No sooner than George blessed the food, Minta took over. "I know we were all together last night, well most of us were all together last night," she darted her eyes towards James and Scarlett and continued, "But I called everyone here because our family is under attack, the enemy is trying to attack my family and I'm not having it."

Cole threw his head back and with a mouth filled with food said, "Attack Ma? Sounds kind of dramatic don't you think?"

"No, I don't think so at all Cole. The bible says the weapons of warfare are not carnal but mighty through God to the pulling down of strongholds.[3] Now, I'm going to do my part and fight that dirty rascal the way I know how to do and that's in prayer but I called everyone here this evening so as a family, everyone can know what we are up against."

Minta's words were not the best for a family dinner discussion however James took the bait and asked, "So what is the family up against Minta?"

---

[3] **2 Corinthians 10:4**: *"For the weapons of our warfare are not carnal, but mighty through God to the pulling down of strong holds;"*

Minta looked over at Travis and asked, "Would you like to tell them or should I?"

Travis tossed up one finger, dismissing himself saying, "I need to use the restroom so you can tell them."

Everyone smirked and said in unison, "Uh-huh, the restroom."

Derrick playfully slapped Travis across his back as he walked past saying, "Don't fall in...you know, while you are in the bath-room."

When Travis cleared the kitchen, Minta filled the family in on Travis' houseguest and how she found out about her.

Marissa looked up from the table and asked, "Is that the girl who was here last night?"

Minta confirmed Amira's presence and said, "Yeah that was her with her long and leggy looking self, looking like a contestant in the Miss Chee Chee Island pageant."

Everyone laughed at Minta's description.

Rena sneered, throwing her hand up, "Who knew? Here I was thinking the boy was gay but instead he's laying pipe while on vacation. Okay then Travis."

Rena's comment stopped everyone in their tracks. She looked around and said, "Now come on, I can't be the only who thought that about him."

George defended Travis by saying, "Rena, how could you think that, he's with Stephanie, he has a girlfriend."

Rena finished chewing and said, "I'm not saying this to be mean but you all know they say those kind of guys get pretty girlfriends."

Travis had been standing on the other side of the wall eavesdropping. He walked in with a twirl and said, "I heard y'all talking about me, hated it...two snaps and around the world, that's right tell-a-friend."

The family erupted in laughter. George commended, "Travis, you crazy boy, just plain old crazy."

Derrick chimed in and said, "Speaking of Stephanie, does she know about this?"

Travis quickly answered and said, "No she doesn't and I'd like to keep it that way."

Minta followed up behind Travis by saying, "I hope she doesn't find out because her parents are dear friends of ours. This would not look well for us if they found out."

Cole stood up and said, "Hey bro, it sounds like you put it on this girl, you got chicks following you across International waters."

Minta stopped the brotherly banter and said, "Sounds like he not only put it on her but he also put it in her too. Especially if she is indeed pregnant with his baby. You know what, this girl strikes me as more of an opportunist than anything."

Scarlett didn't understand how Travis' situation would rise to the level of Minta calling a family dinner so she started up a conversation with Marissa to trade pregnancy stories.

"Marissa, mom tells me you haven't been feeling well. What's going on, what have you been feeling like?" Scarlett asked.

Leaning back in the chair, Marissa responded, "Cole and I stopped at a restaurant on our way here for Travis' party and I think I may have gotten food poisoning or something. I haven't been able to keep anything down and I feel achy like."

Pushing her food around on her plate, Scarlett asked, "Do you think you should go and get checked out while you're here? I mean, James is a heart doctor but he could probably get you in to see someone at the hospital if you wanted."

Rubbing circles around her belly, Marissa said, "I think I may do that because I don't really want to take anything and truth be told, I'm starting to feel worse. So maybe after dinner? Can you see if James can arrange something?"

Scarlett gave Marissa an easy nod and said, "You bet, we'll get you squared away. Mommy needs to feel better so we can make sure my little niece or nephew is safe in there."

The indistinct chatter continued around them until Scarlett heard her name called.

Minta moved on from Travis to inform the family of the latest tales from Carson Montgomery.

Learning that two of his children were in the middle of serious issues, George lashed out, "Why am I just now hearing about any of this?"

Minta tried to offer an explanation, "George, everything was happening so fast. You were out golfing and I figured you'd find out soon enough."

George deepened his tone and said, "You should have called me."

Rena and Derrick pulled James aside to ask him about the details of Carson's petition.

Scarlett folded her arms over her stomach, she sat with an unfocused gaze, shaking her head thinking, *I don't know why my mother has this intense need to be right. She wants to make sure everyone knows she was right about everything. This is what this whole dinner is about. She wants to prove I wrong about Carson and how she told me not to trust him and honestly, I have no idea why she's so upset about Travis.*

Minta had always spoken her mind, she would say whatever she felt necessary even if it was unpopular and sometimes hurtful.

Looking at George she said, "The important thing is you know now and we all need to figure out as a family what we intend to do. The way I see it, I want to tackle these issues before they become bigger issues."

Feeling dismissed, George sat down distancing himself away from his wife.

In true Minta fashion, she started with the backhanded comments, "I've been thinking about this all day and it seems to me for the first time I realized that Travis and Scarlett are actually brother and sister, cut from the same cloth." Minta began to categorize Travis and Scarlett into a "type", the selfish type, the ones who only thought of themselves. "I don't see how you all didn't use better judgement. Have you guys even thought about these children and the unborn children that will be brought into this world? Have you given any consideration as to the impact your decisions will have on them? These are innocent children we're talking about here. What about them?"

If Travis and Scarlett were cut from the same cloth, their common denominator would be George although Minta hadn't quite thought that through when she made the comment. Nevertheless, the remark slit George in two, the power behind her words cut deep.

For George, he had a sense that time seemed to have stopped, better yet, time rewinded for him. Spots flashed in his vision and he trembled in his limbs.

"How dare you Minta. Who are you to judge Travis and Scarlett, anybody for that fact. I'm about sick and tired of your holier-than-thou attitude. You walk around here bible quoting and bible toting but you are the most hypocritical person I've ever met?"

Everyone in the kitchen sat in disbelief. No one had ever heard George speak to Minta in such a manner. She stood with a hard jaw line and a jutted chin.

George continued his tirade, "I've seen you make snap judgments about people without any consideration. You put more focus on being right than be relational. What gives? I've taken about as much as I can." George's bottom lip began to tremble. "I feel like I'm suffocating around you with your sanctimonious performances. You and I both know this is all an act. Somehow you think pretending to be God's right hand, that'll earn you forgiveness for cheating on me."

George's revelation sucked the air out of the room. Cole stood to calm George and he threw his hands up to keep Cole from coming any closer. The family was paralyzed by George's exposé, their mouths dropped open and their7 eyes bulged.

Minta blew out a breath that rattled her lips. Her eyes narrowed in on George as if she was aiming for a target. She strolled out of the kitchen in a way signaling George wasn't worth her time or energy.

Chapter 17

Mother Montgomery arrived at the Bolts, the Bolton family inn. She stepped into the foyer and asked, "Hello there, may I ask, who is the manager on duty this evening?"

Satisfied with the response from the front desk clerk, she asked to be seated for outside dining. It was customary for the manager to greet their guests, the charm of the sisters added to the fascination of the inn. Mother Montgomery figured she'd enjoy a nice meal and handle business at the same time.

The cuisine at the inn was legendary and exquisite, guests traveled from around the world to sample the mouthwatering, seasonal, and sustainable local creations. Sitting atop watching panoramic views of the rolling hills and vineyards added to the experience one would enjoy at The Bolt.

Making the rounds to all of the inn's dinner guests, Delores caught sight of Mother Montgomery. For a brief moment, she considered not going over but then she thought better of her decision and followed through.

"Good evening ma'am, did you enjoy your dinner tonight?"

"Well hello there, I wondered if you were going to come over. You looked like you weren't sure and yes, compliments to the chef, my dinner was delicious. Will you please sit and join me for a moment?"

Hesitating, Delores said, "I really need to continue making my rounds."

Mother Montgomery gave Delores a sharp look and said, "Go handle your business dear; I don't mind waiting."

Delores shifted her weight from one foot to the other, she offered Mother Montgomery a quick, false smile and conceded, "I have a few minutes, what do you want."

"Just like I thought," Mother mocked. "So how's your sister doing, things okay between you two?"

Shrugging her shoulders, Delores fired off, "She's fine I guess, why are you asking about her?"

Amused by Delores' apparent defiance, Mother wiped the corners of her mouth and folded her napkin in her lap, chuckling and said, "Bless your little heart."

She leaned in closer to Delores and asked, "Do you have any idea how your sister spent her afternoon?"

"Today is her day off and I haven't seen her since this morning so no, I don't know how she spent her afternoon ma'am. Is this going somewhere because I would like to get back to work."

Mother Montgomery looked around at her fellow diners and said, "Oh this is definitely going somewhere. I need you to understand something, see because, I came to you and apologized. Do you remember that? I even told you my son needed you and yet, you did nothing. I told you how women are practically throwing themselves at him and I also told you how much I hated it but then again, you still did nothing."

Delores fidgeted, tapping her fingers on the white linen table cloths, she exclaimed, "We aren't teenagers anymore can you please tell me what expected me to do?"

"I expected you to reach out to him or if he reached out to you, I wanted you to embrace him. But you didn't."

Mother pulled her phone out of her purse. She followed the directions Jason had given her earlier and said, "See, you think I'm playing games but I want you to see something."

Playing the video, Mother Montgomery watch Delores with clear intentions as she stared at Mother Montgomery's screen.

The more Delores watched the faster her eyes began to blink. Delores' mouth opened, she started to say something but she couldn't so her mouth closed. *"What is Dottie doing? Is she crazy? Better question, why is she doing that?"* Delores thought. Delores realized the church could have had Dottie arrested but didn't, her quick, darting glance to Mother Montgomery expressed a hidden thanks.

Mother folded her arms across her chest and said, "Now see here, let me tell you something. You are allowing a grudge against me keep you from being with my son and in the meantime he's being exposed to all types of female piranhas. Your sister being one of them, no offense. Now tell me, what are you going to do about this? Not that you need my permission but you definitely have my blessing to see about him. He needs someone he can trust; someone he can talk to. He has a lot on his plate and he needs a good woman in his life and I can promise you it ain't none of these fluzzies walking around here, Delores, I'm going to say it again, he needs you. I pray you hear me this time."

Delores stood from Mother Montgomery's table, carefully pushing the chair under the table and said, "Your dinner is on the house tonight."

Chapter 18

Marissa, Cole, Scarlett and James walked into the hospital. James was able to call in a favor with one of his colleagues who was willing to see Marissa.

Rena and Derrick had taken Chandler home with them.

Everyone disbursed from Minta and George's house faster than a toupee in a hurricane. It was apparent the episode between the couple was weighing heavily on their children. There was an over-the-top attempt to avoid discussing what had transpired.

Inside the examination room, James' coworker, Dr. Simone Hale came to greet the foursome.

Dr. Hale began asking basic questions based off of Marissa's intake questionnaire.

"So Marissa, it says here you feel like you may have eaten something that didn't agree, like you may have food poisoning and you feel achy, like the flu?"

Marissa acknowledged the doctor's questions and offered more details about her symptoms.

Cole stood close to Marissa rubbing his hands through her hair. He leaned in and kissed her on the forehead.

Dr. Hale was quite intuitive, she possessed a unique ability of discernment which led to her being such a great doctor. She was oftentimes deeply attuned to her patients and highly empathetic to their conditions.

"I'm going to order a few tests, we'll need to draw blood and I'd like to send you down to have a sonogram as well. Is that okay Marissa?" Dr. Hale asked.

Marissa answered and offered more symptoms, "Yes, Dr. Hale that sounds fine but I'm starting to feel kind of queasy, I'm feeling real nauseous right now."

Dr. Hale began to proactively make changes as she began to assess and observe Marissa's body language. In a sweet voice she asked, "Marissa, can you lay back for me and lift up your shirt?"

Marissa laid back with her hands folded behind her head.

Taking out her fetal Doppler, she warned Marissa of the cold gel that would cover her stomach. Dr. Hale searched around and heard nothing. She continued to search in various areas around Marissa's round belly and yet she could not locate a heartbeat.

"Marissa, have you been able to feel the baby moving yet?" Dr. Hale inquired.

Marissa lifted her head up and said, "I've been waiting for it but I hadn't felt it yet. Is everything alright Doctor, is the baby okay?"

Dr. Hale offered Marissa comfort, "I'd like to switch the order of the tests and have you go see the sonographer. Actually, I'll have someone meet you down there to draw your blood so you can do both while you are downstairs." Holding up the Doppler, Dr. Hale said, "Sometimes it can take a while to pick up something on these things so I'd like to get a more accurate reading from the sonogram."

While Dr. Hale hadn't given any reason to be alarmed, James recognized her tactics. He was all too familiar with them. He placed his hand on Scarlett's shoulder and squeezed it.

"James and I will wait here for you guys, okay?" Scarlett said as they wheeled Marissa out of the room.

Standing to face James, Scarlett laid her head on his chest and asked, "What do you think is going on? Do you think everything is okay with the baby, I mean, I think my heart nearly stopped when she couldn't locate the baby's heartbeat."

Rubbing Scarlett across her back, James said, "I'm not sure baby, I'm not an OB-GYN, which is why I contacted Priscilla because she is and she's the best in the business. She will make sure Marissa is well taken care of."

Scarlett stepped back away from James and said, "You may not be an OB-GYN but you are a cardiologist, you specialize in hearts so…"

Pulling Scarlett back in, James wrapped his arms around her and said, "Yes, you are right but listen, like Priscilla said, Dopplers don't always pick up on fetal heart tones and I think she made the right move in sending her to have the sonogram done. If I know Priscilla like I think I do, she's running every test known to man, she very thorough. She'll probably have them attach her to a fetal heart monitor as well to check things out. Now come on, lean on your husband; I don't want you getting worked up."

Scarlett shook her head and said, "Speaking of getting worked up, oh my God, what in the world happened between my parents?"

James sat down and motioned for Scarlett to sit on his lap, he folded his arms around her stomach, "Whew, that was like witnessing what World War III will look like. Did you know about the -."

Scarlett interrupted James before he could finish his question, she held up her hand and said, "No, and don't even say the word. I had no idea but a lot of things are starting to make sense now."

James ran his fingers up and down Scarlett's spine as if his fingers were climbing a staircase, "What do you mean sweetheart?"

Scarlett allowed her head to fall back, "I don't know, I mean, growing up, I never had any doubt that my dad loved my mom. For as much as I could tell, he adored her but then there would be times I would watch them together and things just didn't seem right between them. I chalked it up to living life."

Speaking in a soft tone, Scarlett said, "I've never seen my dad like that. When he said that in front of us, I don't if you saw it but he had a strange look in his eyes. He's always been the protector, he has been our family's protection for ever and tonight, he left my mother exposed."

James tried to extend reassurance to his wife, "That just goes to show sweetheart that you never know what people are going through. But you know what, George is a good man, he's a decent man who fell prey to a weak moment. It happens to the best of us. Minta is strong, I'm sure right now, they are both hurt, angry, and upset but I believe, they'll get through this."

An attendant wheeled Marissa into the examination room and Cole followed behind.

Both James and Scarlett stood, "Did you get to see the baby? What did the sonogram show?"

Clinging to Marissa and gazing around the room without looking directly at Scarlett and James, Cole said,

"They wouldn't tell us anything. The girl just kept saying, the doctor will discuss your results."

James stooped down by Marissa and said, "How are you feeling now Marissa?"

Marissa held up a thumbs down.

"Poor thing threw up twice while we were down there." He reached over and grabbed the wastebasket and sat it down next to Marissa in case she needed it.

Cole denied the fear trying to creep up on the inside of him, he attempted to keep his voice light and encourage Marissa and laud her with praise and compliments, telling her how brave and beautiful she was.

Dr. Hale entered the room.

She signed into the terminal to see if the results from Marissa's tests had been updated on her electronic medical records.

Dr. Hale took a moment to put herself in Marissa's shoes in an attempt to present her with the maximum amount of support she could give.

In a glimpse, Dr. Hale clued James in without even saying a word, as doctors there was a hidden layer of solidarity they understood. James received the hint and stepped closer to Cole and Marissa while steadying Scarlett.

Dr. Hale scooted her stool over to Marissa and said, "Marissa, according to the results of your tests, it appears as if you are bordering being twenty weeks pregnant. Based on the bloodwork, we were able to determine, the source of your discomfort is from Listeriosis, this is a type of food poisoning, so you were correct."

Dr. Hale discussed the details of Listeriosis with everyone, they all listened with intent, holding onto every word that came out of her mouth.

Scarlett reached for her phone and down to the side she did a quick online search. Upon reading the results, she began to tremble and cry. James ushered her outside.

Marissa shot up, "Why is she crying?" She exclaimed.

Dr. Hale took back control over the room and said, "Marissa and Cole, there is no easy way to say this. We have been unable to detect any fetal movements or heartbeats of your baby. I'm really sorry. Normally the baseline for a miscarriage is at anything under twenty weeks and anything over is considered to be a stillbirth. The germs, the infection you contracted from whatever you ate more than likely passed through to your baby and unfortunately you are no longer carrying a viable fetus. I'm really sorry for your loss.

Marissa grabbed the sides of her head and said, "Wait. What? What are you saying? What's happening here? I don't understand."

Dr. Hale held Marissa by her arm and said, "I'm sorry but the baby is dead. I'm going to have to get you prepared for surgery, I'll go in and assist with the delivery of your baby."

Cole climbed onto the examination table with Marissa and held her. The tears she shed carried sound, howling sounds oozed out of her, hearing of no heartbeat caused her heart to ache. Hearing no fetal movement caused her to quake and quiver all over.

James reentered the room. He knew the sight of sorrow and misery, he took off the brother-in-law hat and replaced it with his doctor's hat. Doing so would allow him to keep his emotions in check and be a strong layer of support for the grief-stricken parents. Someone needed to be because Scarlett was a basket case. He'd instructed her to go to the cafeteria and wait for him.

Dr. Hale called to officially admit Marissa into the hospital and to schedule the surgery.

In a flash, Marissa sat up, wiped her face and asked with a shaky voice, "How long before my surgery?"

Dr. Hale sat her hand on top of hers and said, "It'll take about an hour to get everything set up for you."

Marissa looked at Cole and James and said, "That means that for at least another hour, I'm still pregnant." Marissa's voice cracked as the tears streamed down her face, massaging her stomach, she said, "And I want to remember being pregnant."

Cole stopped Dr. Hale and said, "Like my sister and her husband, we were going to wait and find out the sex. Was the sex documented in the sonogram she had earlier?"

Marissa flicked around with her fingers and said, "Yes, I'd like to know who this little person is."

Dr. Hale signed back into the terminal and scanned for the sonogram, she smiled and looked over at Cole and Marissa and said, "Boy." She patted Marissa on her hand and walked out.

The announcement crushed both Cole and Marissa. Even though they asked to know, the words seemed to humanize the situation. A real life baby, created by their love was about to be extinguished.

Marissa cried out, "I'm so sorry Cole, we should have gone to that other restaurant but I wanted to go to the other one. I'm so sorry, this is all my fault. I'm a nurse for crying out loud. I knew it, I knew from the moment the doctor couldn't find anything but I didn't want to believe it. My mind wouldn't let me and it still won't. What kind of midwife am I going to be and I can't even carry a baby without getting it sick?"

Marissa's sobs penetrated through Cole's body, he sat Marissa up and looked her squarely in her face and said, "You stop this right now. Baby listen to me; this is not your fault. You did nothing wrong. Never in a million years would I blame you for something like this. You are still a mother and you're going to be an amazing midwife. You and I have been blessed with an angel baby, our own guardian angel."

James gave Cole a pat on the back and squeezed Marissa's hand, "I'll give you two some privacy, I'll be back to check on you guys later."

Cole called out, "Hey James, can you do me a favor?"

"Whatever you need brother, what can I do?"

Cole handed James his phone and said, "Can you please take a picture of us?"

Repositioning himself back on the table with Marissa, Cole lifted Marissa's shirt and stared at her baby bump for a quick minute. Leaning down, Cole held onto Marissa's stomach and kissed it as if he was holding and kissing his newborn son for the first time.

James captured the tender and emotional moment. He placed the phone on the counter and walked out.

Chapter 19

"We need to talk."

George found Minta in the pool house.

Minta flipped through the pages of her bible, prior to hearing George's voice, her fingers landed the following scripture:

"Do not repay anyone evil for evil. Be careful to do what is right in the eyes of everyone."
- Romans 12:17 (**NIV**)

Facing her husband, Minta knew it would be hard to receive the meaning behind the scripture. It would be hard to understand that those who seek revenge are indeed the ones who are trapped and defeated while those who forgive without hesitation are the real overcomers. It was hard to reconcile that notion through her fleshly desire to inflict pain on him somehow.

Reading the scripture again, Minta played around with a weak smile and thought, *"God, you're funny."*

Looking up from her bible, Minta tilted her head and asked, "And what do you want to talk about George?"

George walking closer to Minta said, "I think we need to talk about what just happened." He'd been mentally berating himself over his public outburst.

Crossing her arms and closing off her posture, Minta used sarcasm and said, "I think you've done enough talking for everyone tonight."

"I know you're angry but so am I. You talk all holy and righteous out of one side of your mouth but you hurt people with your words out of the other side. You make all these snap judgements about people Minta and that's not right. You do all this preaching and teaching but you don't take heed to the messages you preach. What you said to those kids tonight was absolutely wrong. I couldn't help it, I admit, I lost it, what you said sent me to a place I promised myself I'd never go."

Minta scoffed, "Part of the problem is that they aren't kids, they are grown adults who are not thinking and doing dumb stuff."

George held his head down but lifted up his eyes, "People who live in glass houses shouldn't throw stones. The reality of life is that grown adults do dumb stuff, they make bad decisions...i.e., the way I handled myself tonight."

Baiting George, Minta said, "Glass houses huh, George, you told me you forgave me and now I see that's a big, fat lie."

George crumbled under Minta's scrutiny. "You will never understand how I feel. Yes, twenty-five years ago when I said I forgave you, I meant it but there are times I still carry the residue in the back of my mind. Minta, that was like the ultimate betrayal. It's like sometimes it sits there like a ticking time bomb and certain things make it go boom and it explodes."

"You seem to forget that I too had residue but I let it all go. I want to show you something. You see this figurine right here? Over time, it has gotten a few cracks in it. If I were to drop this thing, you'd only be able to see that I broke it. The little tiny cracks and broken pieces already there wouldn't matter. George, you are just like this little sculpture here. You had issues long before you met me and before I cheated but because I did cheat, that's all you can...even after all these years. When we said we were going to work things out, I forgave you for how you treated me early on in our marriage. But you still seem to want to hold on to ancient history. Still to this day you want to blame me for your tantrum you threw here tonight."

Shaking his head, George said, "I still don't see how you can compare the two. Yes, I forgot a few birthdays and anniversaries and yes I worked a lot but Minta, nothing I did should have risen to the occasion of you cheating on me. Even after twenty-five years, the thought of you with another man sometimes haunts me."

Not long after Cole was born, George and Minta went through a tough time where she found herself in a torrid love affair with a deacon at their church.

Throwing her hands up in the air, Minta mocked George, "Oh my goodness, George is still a victim, even after all this time. What about me George, huh? What about me? You knew I had issues with abandonment from not having my father in my life."

Standing up, George yelled, "I didn't abandon you Minta; I've been here with you every step of the way, you, however, were the one that stepped out on me."

George and Minta's demand to prove their points, their side of the story superseded their need to truly listen and understand the other's perspective.

A wounded Minta squealed, "No you didn't physically abandon me but you emotionally abandoned me George. You forgot I was your wife. More importantly, you forgot I was a woman. I longed for you to notice me, to love me. It was like I became invisible to you. Let's not forget, I love how you've become a revisionist of history, you just didn't forget a few events. You stopped pursuing me and putting in the work for us. Sometimes you were downright mean and hateful." Minta's tough exterior started to wear down and crack.

The screams, the shouting, and yelling reverberated and bounced off of the sound-proofed walls of the pool house. Heightened emotions caused them to stand face-to-face to one another. Their passion was high strung and their desire was strong. George reached out for Minta but pulled back. She extended herself to receive his touch upon seeing her, he reached out again. George grabbed Minta and whispered, "I'm sorry for hurting you tonight; I should have never said what I said."

Minta could feel George's heart pound, she could sense his sincerity. She laid her head up on his chest to listen closer. He smoothed his hands down her sides. Interestingly enough their emotional rollercoaster landed them on their patterned love seat with hands flowing from the north, south, east, and west. The created tension delivered them into a realm of sensuality. Their familiarity accelerated them beyond being angry with one another into a sphere of intimacy.

Unaware of what was going on in the outside world, George and Minta sat up with blank stares. Minta realized she was experiencing mixed emotions, deep down, she was still upset with George. However, it wasn't lost on her how they'd just experienced one of most carnal sessions in their entire marriage.

George stood with an unsteady stance, he was a little shaky in his knees. Pulling up his pants, he felt his phone vibrate.

As he was about to speak to Minta, she interrupted him and said, "I'm going to need some time to digest everything that has happened."

George's chest caved in, "You can take all of the time you need but don't take too long because we have other issues at hand."

Minta stood up and smoothed out her dress, walking over to George as he stared at the phone's screen. "What do you mean by that?"

George turned his phone towards Minta and showed her the message from James that read:

"Marissa lost the baby"

Chapter 20

Mother Montgomery arrived home to find Cherie sitting down talking with Bishop and Cayden-James.

"What's going on here?"

Cayden-James stood and kissed his grandmother on the cheek, he loved her so much. To him, she reminded the family of their past, their lineage, she always made it a point to instill family pride in everyone and also encouraged them to hope for a better future and continuing on the Montgomery name.

Cayden-James answered by saying, "Hey there Grandma Montgomery, we are just sitting here discussing the latest."

Mother Montgomery took a seat next to Cherie and said, "Well Miss Cherie, what's the latest?"

Cherie rolled her eyes and said, "The police were here."

"Did they question you my Cherie amour?"

Cherie nodded her head. Cayden-James spoke up and said, "Monica was here when they arrived so they questioned both of them. According to them, they indicated they were working this as an ongoing investigation but they mentioned they needed to speak with Carson because they found security footage of Carson leaving his apartment. I haven't been able to reach Carson and apparently no one has either. I knew it was a long shot but I even called Christian and Courtney to see if they'd heard from him and they hadn't."

Both Mother Montgomery and Bishop had been paying close attention to how well Cayden-James was handling and managing the family crisis. In fact, everyone had been noticing.

Bishop added, "The investigators also mentioned they've questioned everyone that toured with Cherie and that they have no real suspects but I didn't like how they were making insinuations about Carson. That boy needs to let us know where he is."

Mother chimed in and said, "Have you all forgotten Carson gave his wife a book on how to disappear off the face of the earth? If we aren't having any luck contacting him, he could be taking some pages out of the book and getting lost."

Mother Montgomery's words rested on everyone as they pondered her theory.

Touching Bishop on his leg, she leaned in and asked, "How are you feeling son? You doing alright?"

Bishop leaned back and said, "Yes mother, I'm fine. Still trying to figure out what happened earlier but I don't have time to worry about me when there is so much going on."

Mother Montgomery nodded and said, "I know son. Hey fellas, would you all mind excusing yourselves so I can talk to Cherie?"

Cayden-James jumped up and said, "I need to head out anyway, I'm on my way to pick up Ali. Call me if anything happens or changes."

Mother Montgomery teased, "Going to see Miss Ali, huh? You know, I like her."

Tickled, Cayden-James said, "Yes grandma, I'm going to see Ali and I'm glad you approve."

Mother Montgomery crossed her legs and said, "I said I liked her, I didn't say I approved. Grandma need to know more about her before she gets any approvals."

Laughing, Cayden-James said, "Alrighty then, I'm out, bye y'all."

Bishop stood up and said, "Alright well, I guess I'll go and find me something to eat. I think I'm probably going to retire early tonight; I'll see you two in the morning."

Mother Montgomery glanced at Cherie and said, "And then there were two."

Cherie avoided looking at Mother Montgomery. While she hated to admit it, Mother's knack for calling her out angered her but on the flip side, she'd begun to appreciate the wit and wisdom of the guardian of the Montgomery generations. To her family, Mother Montgomery was a constant source of good old-fashioned common sense and stability.

Patting the empty seat next to her, Mother Montgomery motioned for Cherie to move from her chair to sit closer to her on the sofa.

Responding slowly Mother Montgomery said, "Tired of waiting on you, bring your little narrow tail on over here. You need to put some clothes on, got your business all out for everybody to see. Come on over here, I want to talk to you."

Cherie leaned back and swallowed hard asking, "What do you want?" She cringed under Mother's watchful eye.

"Cherie, you are going to keep right on being disrespectful and I'm going to be forced to knock you back into vacation bible school, where you can learn some stuff."

Mother Montgomery inched in close to Cherie and said, "I want to know two things. What all do you know about Monica, will she be attending the young man's funeral?"

Cherie shrugged and answered, "She said she was going and to be honest, I don't know much about her. She's a great manager, I know that. She and the management team keep me booked and I have to say she's been very supportive during these last few days. She knows what it's like to be out on the road so I feel like she understands more of what I'm going through than you guys."

Mother Montgomery nodded and said, "Uh-huh. So what you're saying is, you trust her?"

Cherie responded without thinking, "With my life."

"Okay, that's what I needed to know." Mother replied.

With an expression that appeared painful, Cherie said, "I thought you had two things you wanted to know?"

"Oh yeah, I almost forget. Now tell me, what's up with this so called video you supposed to be in?" It's nasty huh? What's on it?"

Cherie blushed and started to speak.

Mother stopped her.

Mother Montgomery clenched her chest, "Oh Lord have mercy, don't tell me. I changed my mind."

Cherie shrugged her shoulders and attempted to get up, "Okay then, nice talking to you."

Mother tripped Cherie, she stopped her from leaving, Cherie stumbled and fell back onto the sofa. She looked at Cherie and said, "I bet you probably on there with your butt all tooted up aren't you and didn't you say several people was in it? Tsk-tsk, y'all just nasty. What were y'all doing Cherie, you can tell me, I wasn't saved all my life."

Cherie stood up and said, "And on that note, I'm out of here. But before I leave, according to Monica, there is no need to worry, the video has been destroyed."

Chapter 21

"Travis, how long are you going to keep me cooped up in this apartment?"

"I'm sorry Amira, I was on my way over there but I just got a call about a family emergency and I'm not going to be able to come right now."

Huffing, Amira pouted over the phone, "Travis, that's not fair. You promised. You told me you were going to come back so we could talk and now you're standing me up...again."

Rubbing his forehead, Travis lowered his head, "Amira, please. My family needs me right now."

Shooting back, Amira yelled, "I need you right now Travis."

Pulling the phone away from his ear, Travis, "*This chick is crazy.*"

Travis felt Amira was hindering him from meeting up with the family. He was about to speak when she interjected an idea.

"Travis, I have an idea. How about you come and get me and then you and I can go see about your family together. Sounds good right?"

Clenching his jaw, Travis bared down on his back teeth, "Amira, I'm clear across town, too far to come get you and go where I need to go. I will however pick you up tomorrow, my family would like to officially meet you. I know you've been wanting to meet everyone, I told them about you and they'd like to have dinner with us."

Travis's words worked like magic, he was able to turn Amira's attitude into grin that couldn't be contained. She repeated over and over, "Wow, I can't believe they really want to meet me."

Checking his watch, Travis started his car again, he'd pulled over when Amira started yelling. His thoughts were scattered, more than anything, he wanted to be surrounded by his family and friends and Amira was keeping him from doing that.

With the hospital in sight, Travis tried to appeal to Amira, "So listen, I've been making sure food is being delivered to you. I brought you some snacks when I went out for breakfast this morning so you shouldn't be hungry. I have an extensive movie library so help yourself to that and I promise I'll touch bases with you later."

Amira blew a kiss over the phone and said, "Okay Travis and you better not forget me here. You should know, I can't be held responsible for what I might do when I'm feeling neglected."

Pulling into the hospital's parking lot, Travis put on a happy face as he spotted a familiar one. He hurried up with Amira and said, "I won't forget and I'll talk to you later."

Hanging up his phone, he heard a knock on his window. He opened the door and smiled. He reached out and embraced Stephanie and kissed her on the check, thanking her for joining him at the hospital.

Stephanie looked Travis over, "Before we go in here, are you feeling better? It's only been like a day but I feel like I haven't talked to you in a long time."

Travis leaned in closer to Stephanie and said, "That's my fault and I'm sorry, it's been a long day and you are so amazing to care about me and my family. I really appreciate you being here with me."

Stephanie grabbed Travis' hand and said, "There is no place I'd rather be."

For a moment in time, they lost awareness of their surroundings. The two stared at each other briefly, relishing in their feelings for one another. The roaring sounds of an incoming ambulance brought them back to reality, reminding them why they were at the hospital in the first place.

Travis' nervous giggle clued Stephanie in to his feelings of anxiety concerning visiting with Marissa and Cole. He backed up against his car and asked, "What do I say to them? What do you say in times like these?"

Stephanie stepped closer to him and grabbed his face and said, "Sometimes saying nothing and being present is enough. Right now, there are no words. Most of the time when people don't know what to say they end up saying the wrong thing so let's just be here for them."

Travis' face went slack, he reached in and kissed Stephanie, he whispered, "You are just too good to me. Thank you for being here."

Chapter 22

"Good morning my dear sister."

Delores looked up over her coffee mug as she offered a weak, "Good morning."

"You sleep okay last night?" Dottie asked buttering up a biscuit.

Delores placed her mug down, she placed her folded fingers down on the table and said, "Actually I didn't get much sleep last night Dottie." Her eyes were cold and hard as she watched her sister eat without an apparent care in the world.

Sneaking a peek at the picture she'd taken with Bishop the day before, Dottie said, "That's too bad, I slept like a baby. I feel great today, like things may be working out in my favor."

Using a careful and controlled tone, Delores said, "Working out in your favor huh? You think taking pictures of drugged up men will make things turn in your favor? I don't know what you were thinking Dottie."

Dottie's thoughts centered on the facts of what her sister was saying, she couldn't believe it, "*How does she know?*" she thought.

She scrambled to find a reply, the only thing she could come up with, "I have no idea what you are talking about."

Delores slammed her hand on the table and shouted, "Don't play dumb with me, they have you on video. How could you Dottie?"

The aftertaste of Dottie's fluffy biscuit turned into a sour taste, her cheeks burned and tears pooled together behind her eyelids. "You have no idea what if feels like to be me. All of our life, everyone has always favored you and forgetting about me. I grew up feeling invisible, like I was always your shadow. I just wasn't in your shadow; I was your shadow."

Delores did a double take, "Dottie, what on earth are you talking about?"

Dottie continued on, "You've always gotten what I wanted, even who I wanted. People would say, Delores, she's the prettier twin. How could they say that when we are identical," Dottie screeched. "He was enjoying coming out here and eating with me. You told me you didn't want him so I figured this could be my chance. I've loved him since we were in High School and for whatever reason, he chose you instead. Now that Regina's gone, he's lonely and I figured if he kept spending time with me then maybe he'd choose me this time."

Clapping her hands, Delores hollered out, "Bravo, bravo. What an act, you should get an award for that performance girl. I think it's funny how you are now trying to blame me for all of your problems. I'm sorry you feel like my presence caused you pain in any way; I don't remember it like that at all."

Dottie rose up and said, "I would have had him if it weren't for you."

Delores stood up over her sister and yelled, "Dottie, you are delusional if you think you can make him choose you. I don't get why you would go to such lengths to try and get a man? We aren't in High School anymore Dottie, you need to get a grip. In fact, can I ask you something, what were you even planning to do with those photos?"

Dottie didn't answer because she hadn't gotten that far in her planning. For the time being, she was simply enjoying looking through the photos of them together, even if he was unaware he was in the pictures.

"Do you realize what Wondrous Works could have done to you?"

Dottie zoomed in on her sister "How did you find out about this, does he know what happened?"

"You are always worried about the wrong things. It doesn't matter how I found out, just know that I did. As far as I can tell, he doesn't know what you did.

Cursing under her breath, Dottie said, "I need to tell you something."

Clearing her breakfast dishes away, Delores snapped and said, "Dottie, I really don't want to hear anything else you have to say."

Dottie bent her neck forward and said, "You need to hear this."

While Delores didn't sit back down, displaying a stiff stance, she did stay to hear what Dottie had to say.

"I've been offered an opportunity to consult on an inn in Michigan. Everything has checked out and now, I think I'm going to go." Dottie's voice dropped off and then went quiet.

Looking past Delores rather than looking at her, Delores said, "Whatever Dottie."

"If I leave, that'll leave you in charge of keeping everything around here," Dottie replied."

Delores walked out and slammed the door with more force than necessary.

Chapter 23

Mother Montgomery sat with her eyes closed meditating in the family prayer room, a room she visited daily. The worship music played softly in the background and she held one hand to her chest and the other to her bible. The current state of her family was in a mess and she needed to connect with the source of her strength, the light of her life.

She administered her daily communion and began to talk to the Lord. She prayed:

"Father, God in heaven, You sit up high and look down low. You know all about us and what we are going through. You know us all, one by one and name by name. In all my days, I've never known you to fail. Lord, down through the years, You've been so good to me; I just can't tell it all. Father, You've let us know in your word that the Holy Spirit searches the hearts of man, meaning, He can search the hearts of the entire body of Christ and represent us all before Your throne.[4] You are just that kind of God and Lord I thank You that I can come before Your throne of Grace where I might obtain mercy and find grace to help me in my time of need because Lord I need you right now[5]. Lord, my family needs You right now, each and every one of us Jesus. I thank

---

[4] **Romans 8:26-27**: *"In the same way the Spirit also helps our weakness; for we do not know how to pray as we should, but the Spirit Himself intercedes for us with groanings too deep for words; and He who searches the hearts knows what the mind of the Spirit is, because He intercedes for the saints according to the will of God."* **(NIV)**

[5] **Hebrews 4:16**: *"Let us then approach God's throne of grace with confidence, so that we may receive mercy and find grace to help us in our time of need."* **(NIV)**

You Lord I can look to the hills from whence cometh my help and I know my help comes from the Lord. I know my family's help is going to come from the Lord.

Tears flowed from Mother has she prayed some in the understanding and in the spirit.

She quickened from the stirrings within her spirit. She rocked back and forth and raised her hands in complete submission. She continued to pour her heart out to the Lord:

"Lord, I need You to send Your power down, I need You to make every crooked way straight. Heavenly Father, I'm praying for You bring light where there's darkness and truth where there's deception. Lord, I need You to touch every situation facing my family, I'm putting my trust in You Lord. Heal our hearts Lord and keep us in Your loving care. Father, we can't make it without You. I don't even want to try making it without You. Lord, the devil is busy but greater is He, I'm not worried with that rascal, he's a defeated foe and under my feet."

Bouncing her foot up and down, Mother felt a peace come over her, once she was quite familiar with, she was confident in her prayers, she knew they weren't going up to the ceiling and bouncing off.

Mother Montgomery closed out her prayer saying, *"Father, I believe I receive when I pray. Therefore, Father, I thank You for all You are about to do. I have prayed the word back to You and I've prayed the prayer of faith, believing my prayers avail much. I trust You Father, I love You, and I bless Your holy name. In Jesus' name I pray, Amen."*

Inside the jewel-toned prayer room, Mother Montgomery concluded her time of fellowship by singing songs unto the Lord. She sang and clapped to one of her favorites, the words welled up in her mouth, "*When peace like a river, attendeth my way, when sorrows like sea billows roll; whatever my lot, thou hast taught me to say, it is well, it is well, with my soul.*"

Chapter 24

"Ali, I'm glad you decided to come along with me to this meeting at the prison. Oh and Ali, I had some sweet dreams last night, I was dreaming about those delicious brownies all night long. I think I tasted a bit of heaven when I bit into those brownies."

Blushing, Ali said, "Well, I'm glad you liked them and after you told me about your new idea, I still would like to be a part so...I'm here. I think I can still use this program to my benefit because maybe I can learn a little more about the psyche, maybe understand the psychology behind why some people commit crimes."

Ali and Cayden-James walked inside the prison where they walked through several security checks. Cayden-James remembered all too well what it was like to be locked up, he was grateful he'd be able to leave after his meeting. He and Ali were escorted to the Warden's office.

Extending his hand, Cayden-James said, "Good morning Warden Peterson, thanks for taking this meeting with me sir. This is my colleague, Ali Joyner, she will be joining us this morning."

Warden Peterson invited Ali and Cayden-James to have a seat in the two seats in front of his desk. He sat down and said, "Well Mr. Montgomery, when I read your proposal, I was quite impressed. We have a lot of partners for prison ministries and re-entry programs but for some reason, yours stood out to me. I'd like for you to tell me more about it."

Cayden-James loosened the button on his sport coat, "It would be my pleasure to tell you more. As you know, I, myself did some time. Fortunately for me, I have a family that has means and resources, unlike a lot of the people that come out of prison. I believe through Christ, anything and everyone is redeemable. The program I'm proposing will seek to bring forth and consist of a symbiotic relationship between spiritual and socioeconomic issues. I'd like to show these men a different way. By me showing these men how to harness their abilities into something positive, a way to show them how to provide for themselves and their families legitimately, my service to them will be a form of worship and spiritual growth for not only myself but for them too."

Cayden-James was selling himself and his program and doing a fine job. Both the Warden and Ali were highly impressed.

Pointing towards Ali, Cayden-James said, "Ali here is studying to be a psychologist and she will be contributing a significant portion of her field work to this program as well. I'm lucky to have her on board."

Ali's skin was flushed as she listened to Cayden-James speak about her.

Warden Peterson stood up and said, "I'm going to take your proposal and presentation under advisement with our board and I will be back in touch with you as soon as I hear something. How does that sound?"

Cayden-James glanced over at Ali and smiled saying, "That sounds great, I appreciate you taking the time to meet with us and I look forward to hearing from you soon."

Exchanging parting handshakes, Ali and Cayden-James walked out of the Warden's office.

Once outside, Cayden-James blew out an enormous sigh of relief asking Ali, "How do you think it went, how did I do?"

Feeling proud, Ali said, "Dude you were awesome, he'd be crazy not to sign you up as one of their vendors. If they, no, not if but when they call you, it's going to be great working with you on this." With a soft touch, Ali placed her hand on his arm and said, "I'm excited."

Cayden-James tingled at her touch, he became hyper-aware of his body parts, clueing him in that he was indeed very much attracted to Ali.

Looking down and using his portfolio to cover himself, he got a little tongue-tied and said, "Um, yeah, I'm pretty excited too."

Chapter 25

"Stephanie, dear, can you let Cole know we'll get started in about fifteen minutes."

Minta wiped down her countertop for the fifteenth time, she was a knot of nerves and burning off the nervous energy seemed to keep her sane.

Marissa nodded and said, "Yes ma'am, I'll let him know."

After the news of Cole and Marissa losing the baby, George and Minta put their apparent differences aside and stepped into the system of support they needed to be. Minta thought of an idea to have a small memorial, a farewell celebration for their grandson.

In light of the situation, no one was focused on what had happened the night before.

Scarlett, James, and Chandler walked in with a small tree wrapped with blue ribbon.

Rena lit the last of the blue and white candles as Derrick turned on the music.

Cole and George, one on each side escorted Marissa down the stairs where the family was gathered in the living room.

Minta stood in front of everyone and said, "I'd like for us all to stand around Cole and Marissa as a sign to them that we are here for them. We want you two to know that we have your backs and that we all grieve with you. In the days to come, please don't think you are alone and have to deal with this alone because you don't. We are here to help you not "get over" your loss but deal with it." Minta's voice began to crack, "While we reflect on the loss, we want you to know we stand as a family in love."

George walked over and placed his arm around her shoulders, "Kids, as your mother has said, we are all here because we love you. Marissa, because of the short notice, your parents couldn't make it but they will be here this weekend. Minta and I are honored they trust us to care for you. Cole, my boy, you've suffered a loss but I want you to take care of your wife, stick close to her, love her and be there for her. I know it may be easier said than done but try not to become withdrawn and retreat, remember to turn towards each other."

In a way, even though George was talking to Cole, he was also talking to himself and to Minta.

Cole kissed Marissa on the forehead and nodded towards George to indicate he'd accepted his challenge. He stood and motioned for Travis and Stephanie to sit by Marissa. He walked up and took George and Minta's place.

Rubbing the heel of his palm against his chest, Cole spoke up, his face was puffy and his eyes were red. "Marissa and I want to thank you all for doing this and being here, it means a lot. It shows that little Colton George Watson was loved." Saying his name caused Cole to turn away and pause to regain control. The strength he needed to be strong for Marissa was starting to fade. Taking notice, George, Travis, James, and Derrick all stepped in and hugged him, their male solidarity built him back up.

Cole wiped away his tears and said, "I wrote a poem this morning and before I sit down, I'd like to read it."

Removing the paper from his pocket, Cole cleared his throat and, "I call this, "**Angel Baby**."

> *"You became an angel, earning your wings before you were born.*
> *Your mom and I know you're in heaven but our hearts are still torn.*
> *We never got to know you but today we celebrate your life.*
> *Yes, we will wonder what you may have become*
> *but now Colton, you're dancing to the beat of a new drum.*
> *When I heard your heart had stopped,*
> *I would have given anything to have mine swapped.*
> *I promise I will be strong and take care of mom.*
> *For God has given us angel baby who will wait for us in the great beyond."*

Being the artist he was, Cole created a portrait to represent the poem, he reached behind the wall and grabbed it. He walked over to Marissa and presented it to her.

Minta stood and said, "Before we finish up and have a bite to eat, we still need to do the balloon release and plant the tree. Cole and Marissa, with your permission, in honor of baby Colton, we'd like to plant a tree in our yard. We may not get to see him physically grow up but we will make sure this tree grows tall and strong."

Chapter 26

"Thank you for taking me out to lunch Godfrey."

Godfrey took a sip from his glass and said, "Anything for you my sweet. Not to mention, I wanted to bring you somewhere nice when I would tell you I've book our tickets to destinations unknown...well unknown to you."

"Seriously Godfrey, you think you can keep this a surprise from me until we leave?"

Godfrey listened with intent to Rebekkah showing he was interested in what she way saying, Godfrey believed it was his duty to make Rebekkah happy, even when it required sacrifice on his part.

"Yes honey bunny, you said I could plan a surprise for you and that's exactly what I've done, we are going to have a great time."

Consumed by her own nosiness, inched closer to Godfrey and said, "If you won't tell me where we're going, how will I know how to pack?"

Flexing his muscles, Godfrey replied, "You should leave all the details to your man. Your man here has everything under control. All you have to do is better ready to leave at the appointed time and ready to have fun."

Rebekkah threw her arms around Godfrey and said, "I don't deserve you."

Excited about the upcoming trip, Godfrey was beaming until Rebekkah asked, "How long will we be gone, I've ordered an at-home DNA kit, it's a paternity test you can do at home instead of sending it in to a lab."

Godfrey tapped his fingers on his glass to release negative energy, he rushed his speech and asked, "And how are you going to get a sample from Carson, you know he doesn't want anything to do with you? Plus, from what I can tell, he looks like he's skipped town."

Taking the last bite of her lunch, Rebekkah smiled and said, "The test isn't for Carson, it's for you silly. I was so determined to cash in on Carson by having his baby that I didn't even consider this baby could be yours."

Godfrey choked, his eyes squinted, "Rebekkah, I've told you, paternity doesn't make you a father. If you and I are actually going to give ourselves a shot, the test results don't matter to me."

Willful paternity wasn't the source of Godfrey's concern. He was fully aware depending upon the results, if he turned out to not be the father and Carson was believed to not be the father, things could go real wrong, real fast.

Godfrey's strained voice said, "You have become obsessed with this which is why I know in my heart a vacation is just the distraction we need."

Rebekkah leaned in and said, "I guess you're right, we can deal with this when we get back. For now, I'll get my mind right for a fantastic trip."

Chapter 27

"Hello my brother, it is so good to see you; I'm glad you called me to come out."

Bishop embraced his brother, Claude and they walked inside the restaurant to be seated.

Since Claude and Bishop had reunited and Claude was filling in as Senior Pastor at Wondrous Works, they had been able to bring restoration to their relationship.

With everything going on Bishop felt like he need to talk to someone he could trust, someone who would know how to handle sensitive information.

"Inside or outside gentlemen?" The hostess asked.

The two brothers looked at each other, "It's a gorgeous day out, we'll go outside." Claude responded.

Claude slapped his brother on the arm and said, "So how are you coming along? I talked to mother this morning and she filled me in on everything. How are you holding up?"

Bishop Montgomery shook his head and said, "Is that what you call it, holding up? If that's the case, I feel like I'm doing a piss-poor job. Days when I think I'm making progress; I seem to get another crazy phone call of something else happening. This thing with Cherie and now it looks like Carson may be involved somehow, I don't know man, everything is all jacked up."

Claude was blessed with an uplifting personality that allowed him to find something good to say even in bad situations. He could always find the silver lining when there appeared to be none.

"Well you know brother, He hasn't brought you this far to leave you, none of us. He's a very present help even in our time of trouble." Claude exhorted.

"I know, I know, trust me, it is only by the grace of God I'm making it day by day. The good book says, He'll never put more on you than you can bare, well I can tell you this, He apparently thinks more of I me than I think of myself. I don't know how much more I can take."

Claude believed occasional setbacks were made for more meaningful and satisfying comebacks.

Smiling and pointing a finger up towards heaven, Claude recited, "Yes my brother but in that good book it also says in I Corinthians 10:13 that no temptation has overtaken you except what is common to mankind. And God is faithful; He will not let you be tempted beyond what you can bear. But when you are tempted, He will also provide a way out so that you can endure it. My brother, human beings everywhere are being tried and tested but God is faithful, He's going to provide the family with a way of escape. It is up to us not to get weary by losing hope and giving up but to continue holding on to His unchanging hands."

The Montgomery brothers placed their orders and continued their conversation.

"You know, sometimes as church folk, some of us are professionals at quoting scriptures, we know how to use them to our advantage when we need them. The thing is, if we don't believe that in which we preach, these scriptures mean nothing more than fancy words. It is our faith that gives these words power and the ability to work in our lives. I'm not here to preach to you because I know I'm preaching to the choir here, I just want to encourage you and let you know I'm praying for you and I love you."

Bishop nodded and fist bumped his brother saying, "And I really appreciate that. Much love Claude, much love. Now, there's something I want to talk to you about."

"Well good because I have something to discuss with you as well," Claude revealed.

"Mother has been talking about Regina's Titus two luncheon lately saying she wants to keep it going in her honor. In my opinion, Mother doesn't need to worry herself with this, she's taking on too much as it is but you know how she can be. I don't have a problem with the luncheon per se, I guess what I need to know is, would you mind asking Lillian if she'd assist with the preparations? Regina had a team she worked with in getting everything together but Mother is trying to do it all herself. Will you please talk to Lillian?"

"Without a doubt, but I think Mother may have beat you to the punch. I believe she's already talked to Lillian, but I'll double check."

Bishop blew out a sigh of relief, "That makes me feel better. So what did you want to talk about?"

The food was being brought out when Claude spotted a familiar face walking down the sidewalk. Squinting to make sure, Claude chuckled, "Is that Delores Bolton I see walking towards us?"

Bishop swung his head nearly into whiplash trying to locate Delores. His brother noticed.

"Oh, do my eyes deceive me, are you still carrying a torch for Delores Bolt? Man, I remember you had it bad for her and from the looks of it, you still do."

Bishop's ears warmed over and turned red, "It's not like that, she's a grieving widow, her husband passed not too long ago. I'm just a concerned citizen"

Whooping and hollering, Claude exclaimed, "And so are you, concerned citizen my behind. You two could rekindle on common ground, you have something in common."

With little to no emotion, Bishop carried on, "Come from out of the past Claude. We were so young back then and now too much has happened. It wouldn't be the same."

Claude snapped his fingers to get Bishop's attention, "Look here, I know how you felt about her, this is me you're talking to. Are you trying to tell me if you had a chance with her again you wouldn't take it?"

Bishop snapped back, "I think she's in a different place now, that ship has sailed."

"If that ship has sailed, which ship is in port? Man, we need to find you a new first lady. I promise you don't want to know how many women ask me and Lillian about you. I bet if I told you it would make your head spin. So here is someone you cared for, I see you're answering for her but what about you? Would you take the chance or not?"

Before Bishop could respond, they heard, "It's the Montgomery brothers, hi guys. It has been a long time Claude Montgomery. I can still call you that right?"

Delores was standing on the sidewalk next to their outdoor table looking radiant.

Both men stood to greet her.

"I didn't mean to interrupt your lunch, I just saw you guys and thought I'd speak."

Claude said, "It's no bother at all, I thought I recognized you walking but you know it's been a while and these old eyes of mine."

They all shared a laugh and Claude made an invitation, "Will you join us Delores, it would be nice to catch up with you."

Delores shook her hands no, "You guys continue your lunch, I don't want to crash the party."

Claude insisted, "You know what they say, a party ain't a party till Delores runs through it."

Delores laughed and said, "I'll join you two only if you promise to never say that again."

Delores ordered a drink and soon after Claude excused himself saying, "Will you two excuse me for a moment, I need to take this call."

On his way out, Claude turned to get Bishop's attention, giving him a thumbs up and a wink.

Bishop replayed Dottie's words about Delores not wanting him over in his head, those words kept him from saying any out of his mouth.

The silence was awkward. The air around them was thick.

Delores made the first move and asked, "How've you been?"

"Good and you?"

"I've been good, could be better but good."

"Well, in that case, the same for me too."

The mood was beginning to lighten.

"So listen, one of our guests has given me two tickets to a private screening of his film showing here this Saturday. Is it weird if I ask you to be my plus one?"

"I think it's only weird if we make it weird. I don't see anything wrong with two old friends going to support another friend." Bishop replied.

Delores raised her glass and said, "You're right and I'll toast to that. Two old friends going to support another friend, I like that. I like that a lot."

The clanking of the glasses caused Claude to turn towards their table, seeing them share a toast, he motioned a thumbs up to his brother.

Chapter 28

"Minta, you did a beautiful job with the ceremony today, I hate and I do mean hate you are having to go from that to this." Travis said.

Minta glanced over at Travis and declared, "This is what we do Travis, we do what needs to be done and take care of what needs to be taken care of."

George pulled up to Travis' apartment, James and Travis got out from the back seat, James unbuckled Chandler's car seat and picked him up. George and Minta got out and walked up onto the sidewalk.

Stephanie, Scarlett, Rena and Derrick all stayed at the house with Cole and Marissa.

Travis blew out a series of short breaths in an effort to gain control. George placed his hand over Travis' shoulder and said, "Calm down son, everything will be fine."

Everyone walked up to Travis' apartment where Amira was anxiously awaiting.

Travis knocked.

"Why are you knocking on your own apartment door Travis?" James inquired.

The group shared a light-hearted laugh.

"Man, I'm not trying to just walk up on her. Trust me, I think it's best we knock." Travis explained.

Amira opened the door with a welcoming smile, reeking of perfume she said, "Hello everyone, please do come in. Can I get you all anything?"

"No thanks," they all said in unison.

"Travis, baby, aren't you going to introduce me to everyone? Although, I'm pretty sure I can figure out who everyone is."

Travis pointed to George and said, "This is my father, George Watson and my brother-in-law, James and his son, Chandler, and you met Minta earlier."

Amira was moving about, unable to sit still, she squealed and said, "I've heard so much about you all and it is so nice to finally meet everyone, well at least everyone. Where is everyone else?"

Travis was restless and he jumped up and said, "They couldn't make it, they said to tell you, they'll catch you the next time you come for a visit."

Without rhyme or reason, hearing the words next time transformed Amira into a different person, flinging her head back she scoffed, "Next time, there will be no next time. I'm not going anywhere Travis. Have you not told them our news?"

Travis' hands became increasingly moist from all of the sweating he was doing. He began to laugh in a way that lasted longer than normal when no one had said anything funny.

Amira stood up and folded her hands across her chest, "I don't think I told a joke."

Travis closed his eyes and took in a calming breath, "No you haven't told a joke and yes, I've told them."

Standing up over everyone else, Amira felt as if she was in control of the room and everyone in it.

Minta asked, "When I came over the other day, you mentioned needing my help. I wasn't in the right frame of mind to listen to you but I am now, what may I help you with Miss Amira?"

Amira smirked and said, "So you all think I'm pregnant right?"

Everyone replied, "Yes."

Circling Travis, Amira laughed as she was happy about steering the conversation in the direction she wanted.

Throwing her head back she said, "Well good because I have something to tell you all and it's too bad the others didn't come because they are about to miss out on some good stuff."

"Listen up. I'm not pregnant but I'm without a doubt about to give birth." Amira raged.

Unsure how to respond, everyone sat still, even baby Chandler.

George took the bait, "Well, if you're not pregnant, why are you here and what do you want?"

Entering George's personal space and being rather touchy-feely, she grabbed his headed swaying it around saying, "Georgy-porgy, wouldn't you like to know. What is want is quite simple. I want what everyone wants. I want happiness, I want what you all have. I saw you all visiting my island, all happy and cheery."

For the most part, James had been quite, only observing but he broke his silence and asked, "And you feel like you had to go through all of these extremes to find happiness?"

Looking James up and down, Amira said, "Oh dear brother James if it were only that simple. You see, you haven't seen how extreme I can be. I'm very good at reading people and from the moment I met Travis, I knew he was an easy target. People like Travis makes life for people like me really easy. When I met Travis, he was nervous about being on his first family vacation. He was desperate for attention and love from you all and unsure if he'd receive it. So I, being the kind of person I am provided him with all of the care and attentiveness he needed to feel comfortable. He let his guard down around me and if those pillows could talk."

Travis stood up and gave Amira a warning, "That's enough, you need to stop this."

Amira yelled out, "Travis darling, I'm not stopping, I'm just getting started. Those pillows can't talk but I certainly can and I will if I don't get what I want. You see folks, I know everything about everybody in up in the Watson-Hartgrove/Montgomery clan, Travis gave me all the dirt and I'm sure what I know is worth something to someone."

Minta raised up off of the sofa, "Amira sweetheart, nothing you have on us or think you have on us is news worthy or worth anything for that fact. Your plan in all of this is to try and extort money from an unknown family no one cares about?"

"Oh Minta, Travis was right about you, he told me how self-righteous you are, how you are always preaching and teaching but not taking heed to your own Godly lessons."

Travis jumped in, "Minta, she's lying I never said that about you."

"I know people like you, all of you wear your personal relationships with God as a badge of honor. You make claims about how your faith is so important. Well, I believe I don't care how strong your faith is, everyone has a breaking point. I wonder what it would take to break your faith, Ms. Minta?"

Amira was trying her best to pin the family against each other in an effort to manipulate them into what she wanted.

Walking over to James, Amira lifted Chandler out of his arms and held him close. "No one may want to know about you but I'm sure the Montgomery's would want to know about him."

James snatched Chandler from her clutch, he grabbed their things, and rushed out of the apartment, turning back he said, "Handle this Travis or I will."

The door slammed.

Travis apologized to George and Minta begging for their forgiveness.

Minta moved up as close to Amira as she could possibly get, she was so close, she could feel her breathing, without backing down, Minta uttered, "You can't break my faith but it can sure break you." Keeping her eyes on Amira the entire time, Minta followed James outside.

The door slammed...again.

The only two standing, George and Travis. George glanced at Travis who stood white as a sheet of paper and asked, "Um, Amira, you said you want what we have, you said you want happiness, um, how much do you think it would cost for you to have the kind of happiness you think you want?"

Patting George on the face, Amira said, "See there, I knew there was something special about you George. In order for me to be completely happy, I need $250,000 and a flight out of this God-forsaken town, yep, that's what I want, I'm pretty sure that'll make me happy."

Travis desired to get away from Amira but he needed to know, "You'd go through all of this, hurting me, hurting my family, risking jail for some money?"

Amira turned around slowly, "Jail? Oh, I'm not going to jail."

George raised his eyebrows and said, "It may not be over where you're from but you do realize extortion is illegal over here?"

Amira pursed her lips together in thought, "George, you make it sound so bad. I simply see it as an exchange of friends trying to make one another happy. After you all give me what I want; I will sign a non-disclosure agreement guaranteeing I won't say anything to the Montgomery family about their little prince. I'm sure you guys need to discuss this and I get it, I actually respect it which is why I'm giving you all twenty-four hours to respond to my offer."

With a father's touch, George reached in and placed his hand on her elbow and said, "May I ask you a couple of questions?"

On a subconscious level, Amira received George's touch. It reminded her of the touch she longed for from her parents. Unfortunately, Amira was unable to form the necessary relationships and bonds an infant needed with their parents because at the time of her birth, they were addicted to drugs. Her birth forced them to recognize their addictions and they both enrolled into separate rehabilitation facilities. When they got out and resumed custody of baby Amira they then raised her in an overly strict environment. They thought they were keeping her safe, keeping her from making the same mistakes as them.

"Amira, I've heard what you said but why my family and what makes you think we have that type of money lying around?"

Travis dry washed his hands and said, "I'm done and I'm out of here." He left the apartment, slamming the door, once again.

The slammed door jolted Amira back to reality, yanking her arm away from George, she said, "Nice try George. This really isn't about you or your family, it's more so about an opportunity. When Travis told me about the Montgomery's and I looked them up, I knew I'd hit the jackpot. I've seen how you all live, I know you have it."

George tried once again, Amira's statement stood out to him, "By looking at them thinking you'd hit the jackpot, my question then becomes, why didn't you go to them with this information? I'm going to say it is because you really do care or at least cared about my son. I'm not going to slam the door like the others but I am going to leave now. Amira, I pray you find what you are looking for. My family and I will be in touch."

Chapter 29

"Hello."

"Hey, hey, hey my brother, I'm sorry I had to cut out on you two earlier but I had to run out, one of my first church members called and needed to talk."

Bishop chuckled, "You know I know how that goes. They never told us about this side of ministry in seminary school. If you someone ever wants to know what people are dealing with, come be a fly on the wall during a counseling session."

"Amen brother, you got that right. As pastors, we don't have the luxury of choosing to counsel, it comes with the territory because people bring their problems to us seeking the best advice and counsel they can get. As long as we are pastors, we will always be counselors. Jesus, our example, spent an innumerable amount of time counseling hurting people, he wasn't too big for face to face conversations with those who needed Him. He is a wonderful counselor isn't He? Speaking of counseling, how may I counsel you on getting back on track with Delores?" Claude smirked.

"I'll have you know after you left, she invited me to an event this Saturday, a private movie screening. I can't believe she invited me." Bishop replied.

Claude continued smiling, "It's all in His timing man, all in his timing. If it's meant to be, it will be."

"Yeah, I guess."

"I thought you would be more excited about this?" Claude asked.

"Claude, listen, you have two old friends meeting up to attend a movie screening, nothing more, nothing less. I have no expectations other than to go and see a good movie or hopefully a good movie. Switching gears here, you mentioned earlier you had something to tell me but when didn't get a chance to discuss it. What's going on with you?"

Shifting in his seat, Claude spoke up and said, "This has pretty much been under wraps but I've been working with an exploratory committee because the powers that be feel like I would be a great candidate to run for Lander's seat in the State House. They feel with my political background, prominence as a pastor and civic leader, I could represent the district well and win by a landslide."

Bishop's eyes narrowed, "Are you considering it?"

"I'm beyond the consideration phase, I've accepted their offer. I didn't want to say anything until I knew for certain I'd pass the probe and I did. So what are your thoughts?"

Bishop sighed, "Well you know how I feel about politics, I've become quite cynical to the process. Now, if you win that means you won't be able to fill in for me anymore. That is what that means right?"

"That's why I needed to talk to you. Yes, I know how you feel about politics but you should also remember how I feel. This is something I've always wanted and I've patiently waited for my turn and it's finally here. I was angry for years because I felt wronged by not getting the blessing to lead Wondrous Works but truth be told, since I've been filling in for you, I'm more angry now at myself for wasting so many years and missing out on my family's life. I was hurt...but God knew all along there was another path for me. Now, I went and started my own church because of that hurt and praise be to God, it has flourished and grown but this is my time to do what He's actually called me to do. My brother, you either need to figure out when you are coming back or name a successor because I'm moving on."

Chapter 30

The ride back to George and Minta's was quiet. They all filed out of the car and walked inside without saying a word. Inside, Scarlett and her in-laws were watching a movie.

Minta's purse plopped down on the counter and George tossed his keys in the key basket on the kitchen counter.

James walked in with Chandler and kissed Scarlett. "How'd it go? Did we miss anything?" Rena asked.

James took Chandler and laid him down in the playpen Minta had at her house and motioned for his wife and parents to join him in the kitchen.

"What's up with all the long faces, how did the meeting go with the girl?" Scarlett inquired.

"You should probably sit down." James admonished.

Minta took a sip of water and said, "First of all, how are Cole and Marissa, did they eat?"

Walking down the stairs, Cole answered, "I'm fine and Marissa is asleep, what's up, how'd the meeting go?"

Minta was about to speak but George began talking. "I spent the most time with her and she's a piece of work." From his perspective, George took his time to relay to the rest of the family the details of Amira's offer.

Minta walked over to Travis and sat in front of him. She looked around the room at everyone and said, "Travis, I've done it before but I need to apologize to you. When you first came around, I didn't treat you fairly. You were in search and in need of your family and when we or shall I say when I reacted the way I did, I made you feel uncomfortable. No one here blames you for Amira, we are going to deal with this as a family. I'm sorry and I love you." Minta reached in and hugged Travis.

Minta's transparency stunned everyone.

"My baby is in danger and you don't blame him? Excuse me but I'm not buying the oversharing act, you talked about us to a woman you barely knew because she was nice to you where you felt we weren't?" Scarlett shouted.

"Calm down Scarlett." James demanded.

Exhibiting angry tendencies towards Travis, Scarlett continued to shout, "I will not calm down, someone needs to let him know how his actions, him running his mouth has now put us all in jeopardy. Who does she think she is trying to blackmail us like that and where is this money supposed to come from? Travis, do you have $250,000.00, no, you don't which means, someone here will have to cover for you and your big mouth."

Cole made an offer, "Travis, man, don't listen to Scarlett. Whatever you need, I'm all in. However, you all choose to deal with this just let me know. This is a little more than I can handle right now so I'm going to go back upstairs and be with my wife."

Travis nodded and stood up and walked over to Scarlett, "I'm sorry for putting you and the rest of the family in this predicament." He looked around at everyone and apologized. "My life is much different than it was two years ago, even a year ago. Since I've been around you guys, my life has changed tremendously. I don't think I would be where I am today without you all and I'm truly sorry for this situation. Growing up, it was just me and my mom, I wanted more than anything to have siblings to fight with me and play with me. I can't change what has happened but I can make things right. This might even sound crazy but even though you are angry it makes me feel good to have a sister upset with me. I will make things right between us Scarlett."

Minta put a teapot on the stove, turning around she said, "Do you all remember the excursion I wanted us all to go on while we were at Chee Chee Island but no one wanted to go?"

Everyone nodded.

Lining up tea cups, Minta said, "I decided to go on that excursion, all by myself and remember I came back ranting and raving about my new Chee Chee Island friends? The ministry of tourism over there did a fantastic job matching me up with an ambassador so much so, we still keep in touch, long after the trip."

George rose up and said, "I see where you're going with this."

"Yes indeed George. I will be placing a call tomorrow to my friend, Julian to do some digging of my own to see what I can find out about Miss Amira. Pouring the tea for everyone Minta said, "The island isn't that big, for sure someone knows who she is. Travis, send me everything you know about her."

With a bowed head, Travis replied, "Yes ma'am."

Minta blew on her tea to cool it, "We are going to nip this in the bud before it gets too far out of hand. "Hear me when I say, 'lil Miss Amira has messed with the wrong family."

Chapter 31

"Good morning Monica dear, how are you, this is Mother Montgomery calling."

"Hello ma'am, how are you? I missed you the last time I was at the house."

Mother Montgomery coughed and said, "Yes dear, so I heard."

"How can I help you Mother?" Monica asked.

"I'm calling to speak to you about a few things. First, I heard you left here to attend the young man's funeral, is that right? Did you go?"

Monica paused for a moment and answered, "Yes ma'am I did."

"How was the service darling? How is his family holding up? I've been praying for them you know."

"The service was beautiful; it was well done. His family, they are doing the best they can, considering, they are trying not to focus on the investigation and the details of his death. I'm sure they appreciate your thoughts and prayers."

"You know, I still can't get over how he died, I can't even imagine being covered in bees. How do you think those bees got on him like that? I just think his murder seemed so deliberate and it pains me so to see my grandchildren mixed up in this." Mother Montgomery replied.

"Yeah, I know and according to the detectives, they haven't been able to speak with Carson. Which is unfortunate because he's now considered a person of interest from what I heard. Have you all had any luck contacting him?"

"No, we haven't Monica." Mother Montgomery changed lanes and said, "So listen, you knew the man, he was a part of Cherie's tour, who do you think might've done this to him? Did you know him to have any enemies?"

Monica sat still, she had flashbacks of Blue.

"Hmmm, I'm not sure but what I am sure of is that he apparently made the wrong person made and it cost him his life."

"The detectives mentioned he recently made a large donation to a charity." Monica noted.

"And. Is that a bad thing? I mean, is there somehow a link or connection to how he died?" Mother Montgomery asked.

"Well, they said generally when people make large contributions when they normally aren't benevolent like that, most times the donor is trying to clear their conscious, which is one of the many red flags they are working through."

"Monica dear, you seem to know an awful lot about this investigation."

In a heightened voice, Monica responded, "Well, yes because it's my job. It's my job to know what's going on with my artists, we have a brand to protect which is why I'm keeping tabs on Cherie."

"Speaking of Cherie, as her manager, when are you planning for her to go back on the road, dear?"

Monica released a strong sigh, "With everything going on Mother, we are trying to determine the best time for that. We don't want to lose our momentum within our major markets but at the same time, we don't want to push everyone too soon either. There's a delicate balance here. Blue's death is at the forefront of everyone's mind. I think when his killer is caught, everyone's mind will be at ease and we can move forward." Monica explained.

"I'm sure she'd scream if she heard me say this but I don't think Cherie is in any shape to be going back on the road. She needs to stay put right here until things get worked out. She mentioned she has a lot of respect for you and trusts you completely. I hope I can count on your discretion about this conversation. She needs rest right now, you understand, don't you?"

"Yes ma'am I do and Cherie won't hear any of this from me, however, she needs to keep singing. While she's "resting," she still needs to keep up with her vocal training, we don't need her voice to become stale, if you know what I mean."

Mother Montgomery grinned, "Oh, I know what you mean and I know exactly what Cherie needs. I'll make sure she does the right thing. Miss Monica, you can count on me for that. Hey listen, Cherie talked to me about this so called video, do I understand it has been destroyed, is that correct?"

Monica balled up her fists, "Ugh, that doggonit video. That video has been the bane of my existence. I'm so sorry Mother, forgive me, but to answer your question, yes, the video has been destroyed."

"Do you know if there were other copies and if those were also destroyed?"

"Yes ma'am, all copies have been destroyed."

"Monica dear, since you are in the know with the detectives, do they know about this video that no longer exists?"

"Not to my knowledge Mother."

"Okay darling, well I'm not going to take up too much more of your time, Mother gone let you go now but I appreciate you taking the time to talk to me though."
Monica smirked and offered, "Anytime Mother Montgomery, anytime."

Chapter 32

"Is it wrong that I want to eat your brownies for breakfast? To be honest, I'd eat them all day if I could." Cayden-James admitted.

Blushing, Ali questioned him, "You seriously think they are that good you'd want to have them for breakfast?"

Cayden-James closed his eyes, imagining himself eating one of Ali's brownies, he said, "Ali girl, don't play with me, those things are delicious. My stomach just did a flip thinking about them." Opening his eyes, he said, "My mother wasn't much of a baker but she used to try and bake brownies for us. When I tasted that brownie the other day, I told you I felt like I had tasted heaven. Seriously though, I think it made me think of my mother, not in a sad way but a good one. You know, you actually remind me a lot of her. She would have loved you."

Ali got up holding up a finger, excusing herself.

"Where are you going?"

Without saying a word, she kept walking towards the kitchen.

Minutes later Ali emerged from the kitchen carrying two plates, sitting one down in front of Cayden-James.

Cayden-James' mouth dropped open, "You little stinker, what is this delightful looking creation?"

Unbeknownst to Cayden-James, Ali had successfully snuck in a container of brownies where she'd left them with Clarice.

Smiling, Ali announced, "This is a Clarice and Ali original. Taste it."

Cayden-James picked up his fork and bit into a morsel of scrumptiousness. Clarice and Ali prepared a combination of fluffy eggs, creamy cheddar cheese, and hickory-smoked bacon which was placed inside of a hollowed out brownie."

"Are you kidding me right now? Is there no end to your brilliance? Ali, this is amazing, no let me rephrase, you are amazing. I need for everyone in the house to try this ASAP."

Cayden-James' breakfast celebration was interrupted when his phone rang. He looked up at Ali and said, "It's Warden Peterson."

Standing up, Cayden-James answered the call. Ali stood in front of him with her fingers crossed, praying hands, and she even formed a church steeple.

Without displaying any hints, Cayden-James said, "I understand, thanks so much for calling."

Bouncing around, Ali said, "I can barely breath here, what did he say?"

Cayden-James sat his phone down saying, "Before I answer, I need to have another bite of this."

Ali declared, "Dude, this can wait, me needing to know can't. What did he say? Tell me now or I toss the plate."

"You wouldn't."

"You just don't know but trust me, I would."

In sweet surrender, Cayden-James pulled out the bar stool for Ali to be seated. Sitting next to her he said, "I have good news and I have bad news, which do you want first."

"Bad news first please."

Gathering his thoughts, Cayden-James described the situation, "The bad news is, the program didn't get approved."

Ali's head dropped as she released a heavy sigh.

"According to the Warden, someone on the board brought up this nonsense going on with Cherie, calling my family's reputation into question. All they have is rumors and speculation but whoever this person was seemed to have presented a case well enough to where others believed in his apprehensions about me."

Ali frowned at Cayden-James' response, "If that's the bad news, please hurry up and tell me the good news."

Perking up, Cayden-James conveyed to Ali the other part of his conversation with the Warden Peterson, "It's actually great news when you think about it. When I step out of the way, God just has a way of blowing my mind. The warden said he didn't have enough votes but he was still quite impressed with the program. So, even though we won't be doing the program through that correctional facility, he said I don't need to do it through them, in fact, if I do it on my own or through the church, I won't have to abide by their policies and procedures so I can structure in the way I want. He's offering to recommend the program to a few inmates who are set to be released soon and he said he's in an organization of other wardens and he's going to tell them about it as well. Ali, this is perfect. We have an opportunity to do this how we want and make a real change in people's lives. I couldn't have gotten to this point without you. Ministry isn't for everyone; it can be tough if you let it but I appreciate you for hanging with me on this. It means a lot."

Ali's teary eyes locked in on Cayden-James and she said, "Cayden-James this is great news, congratulations." Reaching in for a congratulatory hug, her lips brushed up against his cheek. Unsure of what to do next, she paused. Was it about to finally happen? This wasn't how she'd imagined their first kiss to be but she decided to take a leap and she went for it. Ali made her innocent slip, intentional. Cayden-James responded in-kind.

All of their combined uncertainties about one another melted away with the warmth of their strong feelings.

Their first kiss, it started out slow and grew bigger. The bigger kiss grew intense and then more intense. With his tongue, Cayden-James traced an outline of Ali's lips while her hands caressed his face.

"Kissy-kissy huh? Stop swapping all that spit in this kitchen. You young people, I tell you, just nasty. I'm supposed to eat here." Mother Montgomery said setting them straight.

Their first kiss was now in the history books thanks to an appearance from Mother Montgomery.

Busted by his grandmother, Cayden-James released Ali from his clutch and licked his smiling lips, "Grandma, I didn't see you there."

"No, you couldn't see me because you all puckered up." Mother Montgomery replied.

Escorting his grandmother over to the table, Cayden-James looked at Ali and asked, "Can you and Clarice make another one of those?"

Completely embarrassed, Ali welcomed the opportunity to escape, "Sure thing." She declared.

"I want you to sit here grandma, I want you to taste something."

Standing close to his grandmother, Cayden-James was caught off guard when Mother Montgomery jacked him up in his chest. "You better not hurt that girl; I hope what I saw was genuine."

Struggling to get free from his grandmother's grip, Cayden-James pleaded, "It is grandma, I promise. She means to much to me for me to hurt her. I hurt her and I didn't even know her and now that I do, I plan to make things right with her. I really like her, no like, I really, really like her."

Eavesdropping Ali smiled before she brought out Mother Montgomery's breakfast surprise. Placing a plate down in front of Mother, Ali said, "Here you are Mother Montgomery, I hope you like it."

"And what do we have here?" Mother Montgomery asked.

Speaking up, "This is something Clarice and Ali made using Ali's famous brownies. Grandma, wait until you try it." Cayden-James exclaimed."

"Maybe if you calm down and stop talking, I could try it." Mother said grinning.

Ali looked over at Cayden-James seeking a look of reassurance from him, he stared at his grandmother asking, "So what do you think? You like it? Dad will probably like to try it too, huh?"

Mother Montgomery popped Cayden-James on the hand and said, "Shut up."

The trio erupted in laughter.

Mother Montgomery wiped her mouth and said, "Ali, I've tasted some things in my day but sweetheart this is delicious. This has that savory-sweet combination I like."

Bouncing from one foot to the other Cayden-James grabbed Ali's hand and said, "See I told you girl."

Mother Montgomery looked up and said, "Cayden-James, did you invite Ali to the luncheon like I told you?"

Shielding himself from a potential blow, Cayden-James confessed, "Ugh, grandma, I forgot. I'm sorry but I can ask her now."

Swatting at Cayden-James, Mother Montgomery leaned in and said, "I can tell her now myself, boy."

Mother Montgomery gave Ali a history on Regina's luncheon and invited her to be her special guest.

Ali quickly replied, "I'd love to come and if you need any help, I'm available."

Taking one last bite, Mother Montgomery looked up at Cayden-James and said, "Cayden-James, if you approve, then I approve." Her words and her wink communicated to Cayden-James, Ali had won over his grandmother.

Chapter 33

"It's always a pleasure to meet with you Minta, it has been a while so I was glad to get your call. So what's been going on, fill me in on the latest."

"That's precisely why I'm here. It's like when you are the strong one in the family and everyone is depending on you, where do you go when you need strength and encouragement?" I needed someone to talk to, someone to help me which is why I'm glad you were available to see me this morning." Minta said.

As a church consultant, Minta had come across an untold amount of ministry leaders. Over the years, some had even become close friends. Dr. Mahalia Middleton, a mental health practitioner, who specialized in Christian counseling due to her dual role as co-pastor to a church with her husband was a trusted advisor to Minta. While Minta's visits were far and few between, she knew her sessions with Dr. Middleton were impactful.

Dr. Middleton started with, "I know it's been a long while since your last visit but you know how this goes. The bible says we are to confess our faults one to another and pray so you may be healed[6]. I want you to loosen up and tell me what's going, why are you here today?"

Minta opened up and replayed the details of everything confronting her family.

---

[6] **James 5:16**: *"Confess your faults one to another, and pray one for another, that ye may be healed. The effectual fervent prayer of a righteous man availeth much."* (**KJV**)

Dr. Middleton passed a box of tissues over to Minta who allowed herself to connect with the emotions she felt arising as she spoke. All of the hurt, the pain, the guilt and sadness she felt gushed out of her.

"You will need to come back because we are not going to be able to tackle everything you just said but in general, I believe just by voicing it and getting all of that out, you are probably feeling better. The other part of that scripture admonishes us to pray after the confession and you know that's how I run my sessions. So let's do that." Dr. Middleton grabbed Minta's hands and began to pray, *"Heavenly Father, we come before you with humble hearts and minds. Oh Prince of peace, You are wonderful counselor and we submit ourselves to you in this session for healing and understanding for my dear sister. In Jesus' name we pray. Amen."*

Minta patted her face and said, "Amen."

Dr. Middleton flipped through her notes and said, "The last time we spoke, we talked about your father and your feelings of abandonment. Allow me to present you with something to think about. Because you can't control your father and his love or lack thereof for you, you try and control everything and everyone around you. You grew up not having any control over your circumstances and as a child, you craved structure. So when you became capable of regulating things, you went in, all in and you haven't stopped. Governance is not what you need right now, gentleness is."

Sniffling, Minta nodded her head in agreement.

Dr. Middleton crossed her legs and said, "Based on human nature, we all have predispositions to destructive behaviors that can alienate us from our family and friends and also stunt our growth. Which is why we should always have a reliance upon God. Listen to me, vengeance belongs to Him, not us. What is up to us is to receive and accept forgiveness and offer forgiveness wherever possible. I think you need to let up on yourself and those around you. Loosen up your halo a little and let theirs dangle a little."

Offering a Minta bottle of water, Dr. Middleton probed, "After all these years, why do you think George brought up the affair and especially the way he did?"

Throwing her hands up in the air, Minta cried, "I have no idea, it seemed all quite random. We haven't talked about that in forever, I guess they really never get over it. I thought he had forgiven me and we'd moved on."

"The question is, have you forgiven yourself?" Someone once said to me guilt is like wearing a sweater in the summertime, it's too hot and you need to take off that sweater of guilt. Minta, you present yourself as an exemplary Christian but the truth of the matter is, you are an example of performance based religion. You believe if you do everything right, go to every service, learn as many scriptures as you can, you will somehow erase those blemishes off your record."

Minta began to sob, the cries overflowed from her soul.

"Here's the good news Minta, I'm sure you already know this but sometimes we need to be reminded. According to Colossians 1:22-23, "Because Christ has reconciled you in His fleshly body through death, you are now presented before Him, holy, blameless and without fault. The accusations against you were nailed to the cross over 2000 years ago when His blood covered your past, present and future sins. You are completely forgiven Minta so just keep in the faith and do not be moved away from the hope of the gospel in which you've heard. Oftentimes people have this misconception about Christians, guess what, we mess up too. My job proves it. The difference is we have a loving Savior willing to take the fall for our mess ups. He did it, it's a finished work. Relieve yourself of the pressure to try and live a perfect, controlled life because you will fail every single time. Minta, I want you to finally grasp there is no condemnation for those who are in Christ Jesus. Stop performing and start living for God."

Taking time to pull herself together, Minta allowed for Dr. Middleton's words to sink in. "I feel twenty pounds lighter, thank you for helping me get that monkey off my back." Minta revealed.

"Minta, with respect to you and George, when was the last time you all did an assessment of your marriage? When was the last time you guys sat down and came up with some common goals?"

Shrugging, Minta replied, "To be honest, I don't know if we've ever done that."

"Here's what I want you to do, things are changing for you two, you both are retired now, both of you are transitioning into a new phase of life and I think it would do the two of you some good to sit down and talk about what's next. To make it special, as a couple, I want you to create an aspiration box. In this box, similar to a vision board, you will write down a list of things you'd like to accomplish as a couple. Depending on what you write, gather together items to correspond to your list. So if taking a trip is one, find brochures on the destination and place them inside. The important thing to note, as you work together towards these new goals and complete them, add another aspiration to the list."

Perking up on the sofa, Minta said, "What a beautiful idea."

Giving further instructions, Dr. Middleton commanded, "When you come back, which I hope will be sooner rather than later, I want you to report back to me how you and George have had a meaningful conversation and I'd like to see a picture of your box. If I know you how I think I do, the Watson box is going to be fabulous. On a serious note, let's never let the box get empty, as a couple, you two should always be working towards something together."

Minta was about to respond when she felt the buzz from her vibrating phone. She thought she'd turned off the volume but she hit vibrate instead. She was grateful for the mistake because it was a call she'd been waiting on.

Gathering her things at a pace of a thousand horses, Minta said with speed, "I'm sorry to have to leave like this, I think my time was almost up anyway but I have to take this call. You've been a tremendous blessing and I'll call and schedule another session soon, I promise. Thanks so much. Bye."

Giving Dr. Middleton no time to respond, Minta was already out of the door. Without Minta, Dr. Middleton said a closing prayer for Minta and her family, made her notes from their session, and turned off her clock.

Chapter 34

"Hey baby, you doing okay?"

"I'm not sure, I'm not real sure how I'm supposed to feel. If I'm honest, I don't feel anything but cold and darkness inside. I feel empty and broken. I feel like a part of me has been taken away, like it's been stolen and I have no way of getting it back."

Cole pulled Marissa closer to him and kissed her on her forehead.

"The farewell celebration was nice today and I really appreciate the family, I just wish we didn't need to have it. It's like my mind can't seem to wrap around how you say hello and goodbye to your child all at the same time. In all of the time I was pregnant, I never considered the intersection of where birth and bereavement might meet." Marissa said.

"Baby, we are going to get through this." Cole promised. "You may not know right now but tell me what you want to do and I'll do it." Cole offered.

Marissa turned over and said, "As best as I've been able to, I've been thinking. I know my parents are set to come here and as much as I'd like to see them, I think I just want to get away for a while."

"You have any thoughts on where you might want to go?" Cole asked.

"No, I don't, haven't gotten that far yet. I don't really care where we go, I just want it to be us and far away."

"I'm sure that can be arranged. Anything else?" Cole inquired.

Marissa turned back over to face her husband, "Actually there is. I think I'm going to take this next semester off from school. I don't want to go back, it would be a waste of time if I did, I don't have the capacity for it right now."

Lightly touching Marissa's face, Cole said, "Whatever you need babe, you can take all the time you need." He leaned over to the night stand and opened the drawer pulling out a lovely journal. "I brought you something." He said.

"What did you buy?"

"I was reading online about ways to support you during this time and out of all the ideas I came across, I thought getting you a journal was a great idea. Since you're telling me you will be taking a break from school, I think this will be a perfect time for you to document your feelings. I want you to write when you're confused, scared, angry and even when you have good days and are feeling happy. I want you to explore your feelings of sorrow and your struggles with readjusting. I've always heard writing to be therapeutic for people and there's no better time to try it out than now." Cole suggested.

A weak smile graced Marissa's face, it was the first in days. "I'll do it and thank you so much for taking such excellent care of me but you know, I worry about you too. You've suffered the same loss I have. Are you okay?"

Cole took a slight pause before responding, "I'm fine babe, don't you worry about me. I've learned to not focus on things I can't control and this is something I have no control over. If what I've been told to believe my whole life is true, my baby boy is not dead, his death is not his end but the beginning of life eternal. I do believe that and I take comfort in that. The bible says to be absent from the body is to be present with the Lord. We didn't lose him; I know exactly where he is. Right now, he's doing better than us. The little guy never knew what it was like nor will he ever know what pain feels like, only love and that makes my heart happy."

Marissa sighed and said, "You are such a good man and I love you. Do you know how soon can we leave?"

"As soon as we figure out where we want to go, we can leave. Why?" Cole asked.

"There's one more thing I want."

"Name it."

Marissa sat up in the bed and began to cry, "I want to have the house cleared of any baby items we have. I don't think I can take going back home without him and then having to see his things we were collecting for him."

Cole's breathing was shallow; he was deeply saddened to see Marissa in so much pain.

"I'll take of everything sweetheart. Now, you still need to eat and stay hydrated and rest up so I'm going to get you something and I'll be right back." Cole replied.

There was one more thing Marissa wanted but she couldn't seem to form the words to communicate them to her husband. In that moment, to say the words would seem like a betrayal. Nevertheless, upon hearing the door close, Marissa opened up her new journal and flipped through the pages, she thought, *"These pages are as empty as I feel. Maybe as I fill in the pages, I can fill my life up again."* Grapping an ink pen from the night stand she wrote her first journal entry entitled: **Colton's Courage**.

Chapter 35

"How was your day today Travis? Have you talked to Amira?"

While leaving Dr. Middleton's office, Minta was able to make the contact she needed with her ambassador friend from the island and she called Travis to invite him to dinner to discuss the details.

Travis' posture was sagging and his neck bent forward, "I sent a few text messages to make sure she was alright, trying to make sure she's not tearing up my place but other than that, I can't stomach the thought of talking to her. This whole situation is mind blowing, it literally boggles my mind when I think about what she's trying to do." Banging his hands up against his head, Travis demanded of himself, saying repeatedly, "How could I be so stupid?"

Minta stopped Travis from beating himself up, literally and figuratively, "Stop it Travis, don't do this to yourself. Hey, things happen, it's called life. My advice to you, see it for what it's worth, learn from it, and move on. No need in you piling up a whole bunch of guilt on yourself, it's not worth it. Look here, my new motto is, #give up the guilt. You can best believe, as I'm talking to you, I'm talking to myself. It's time to give it up, nothing about me should resemble guilt. Now that I have that out of the way, listen, I wanted to have dinner with you to discuss what I found out."

Taking a deep breath in, Travis said, "Good news I hope."

Minta took out a folder she had with her and opened it up, "It all depends on how you look it at. It's great news for us but no so good for Amira. You are never going to believe this."

"What do you mean?" Travis asked.

"Well you know I called Julian, the ambassador over there and he called me back today. Turns out, Amira is considered a missing person over there and her family is desperate to find her, there's even a reward for anyone with information about her disappearance."

Travis' mouth dropped open, the words, "Are you kidding me right now," fell out of it.

Sliding over the folder, Minta explained, "Julian emailed me some of the flyers they have posted over there, pictures of her parents, newspaper articles, a whole packet. Apparently she has some serious mental health issues and she left without her medicine, her parents are very concerned about her safety. Take a look for yourself."

Looking over the documents, Travis said, "So what you're telling me is, I'm not as crazy as I thought but she is crazy as hell? Certifiable even."

"Now Travis, don't you go making jokes, it's only by the grace of God, you and I aren't in Amira's shoes. Mental illness is serious and shouldn't be made light of. It's something we don't like talking about but should. We all could stand to go and talk to somebody from time to time. This girl is in trouble. Let me tell you, as mad as I was at her and trust me, I was mad. I could've slapped fire from her when she picked up Chandler and then again when she got up in my face. Nevertheless, even through all of that, I can see the hand of God being in the midst of this. She could have ended up anywhere with anyone but she's here where we will make sure she gets back home with her family where she can get the help she needs. I can only imagine what her parents must be going through right now. My heart really goes out to them." Minta replied.

"I hear you Minta and you have no idea how much you helping me through this situation means to me. I really appreciate all you and George have done. Thank you for welcoming me into the family." Travis said.

"You're our son Travis and when one of our children need us, we're there." Minta explained.

Travis' muscles stiffened, he couldn't help but wonder about the change he was witnessing with Minta.

During Minta's counseling session she was able to take a realistic look at herself, she accepted her reality and vowed to deal with life as it came. Moving forward, she'd decided to stop working to be right and just receive God's grace to live free from guilt and shame. Her approach with Travis and Amira was an initial manifestation to her new way of thinking and living.

"So what's next? I know you have a plan." Travis remarked.

Minta enjoyed a bite of her favorite dessert, red velvet cheesecake. She opened her eyes and said, "Yes, I do have a plan. I'm coordinating with Julian, he's alerted her parents and as soon as they can get a flight, they are going to fly here to get her. You need to stall some time with her, let her know we've accepted her challenge but we're getting the money together, I don't care what you come up with just tell her something. We need to make sure she doesn't leave. When her parents do arrive, we are going to go over to your apartment like we are there to transact business and then we'll let her parents in. Hopefully things will go well and she'll go back with them without incident."

"Let's hope," Travis said exhaling.

Chapter 36

"Hello beautiful."

"Hey there handsome, how are you? I feel like I haven't talked with you much lately; I miss you so much."

"I know sweetie; a lot has been going on. Hey, I'm outside, you mind if I come up for a bit?"

Stephanie couldn't hang up her phone quick enough, she was standing with her door opened when a winded Travis arrived up to the third floor of her apartment complex.

Breathing heavy, Travis said, "Things have been so crazy this week, running up these stairs have been my only work out."

A smiling Stephanie said, "And here I thought you were running to see me."

Stopping for a welcome kiss and hug, Travis indulged Stephanie and said, "Well of course, there's that, you know I couldn't wait to come and see you."

Walking in hand in hand, Stephanie led Travis to the sofa where she was watching television. "Would you like something to drink or something to eat?" She asked.

Sitting on the edge of the sofa, Travis drew his mouth into a straight line and bit his lip. Tapping his heel, he said, "No sweetie, I just left dinner with Minta."

"How nice, did you guys have a good time?" Stephanie asked taking a seat next to her beau.

Travis felt a slight chill internally, his scalp started feeling prickly, he placed his hand on Stephanie's leg and announced, "We did sweetie but I have something I need to tell you."

Grapping Travis' hand, Stephanie inched closer and said, "This sounds serious, is everything okay?"

Taking his time, from past to present, Travis explained the details of his saga with Amira. While he was nervous, he felt more at ease in Stephanie's presence. He revealed to her his fears, worries, relief, and hopes for the situation.

Stephanie's shoulders loosened, slow and steady, she stood and walked into her kitchen leaving Travis behind with a blank expression.

Looking up, he saw her with a bottle of wine and two glasses. Still quiet, she opened the bottle and poured. Handing him a glass she picked up her glass and said, "Thank you for telling me."

Travis glanced around as if he was looking for more to happen, he thought, *"Is that it, that's all she has to say is thanks?"* He couldn't take it, sitting down his glass he asked, "You're welcome, I guess? How are you so calm about this?"

Stephanie placed her glass next to Travis' and breathed in a deep breath, she looked at him and said, "I've known about Amira for a couple of days, she called me. A lot of what said didn't make sense but I was able to put together enough."

Standing up too quickly, Travis knocked over the half empty wine glasses, spilling wine onto the carpet, he yelled, "She did what?"

In a calm and even tone, Stephanie enlightened Travis about her conversation with Amira.

On bended knees, Travis feverishly tried blotting out the stains saying over and over again, "I can't imagine what you must think of me."

Stephanie looked down on him and said, "You want to know what I think of you? I think you are a wonderful man.

You're genuine and honest and a lot of people can't say that. You are a rare find Travis Raulerson. You apparently had no idea she called so you could have kept this to yourself. The mere fact you came here to tell me this when you really didn't have to shows me you are the type of man I can trust my heart with. Not only that I see a man I couldn't love more."

The "L" word, that was a first for them.

Travis heard her say it and responded quickly, "And I couldn't love you anymore than I do right now Stephanie." Her validation of him meant the world. Her influence in his life allowed him to build up his sense of self-worth and confidence. He realized having her in his life was a blessing he never knew he needed until the day he met her.

Both Stephanie and Travis desired for their relationship to be stronger and more intimate. They'd toyed around with the idea of taking their relationship to another level but tonight there was no playing around. Still on his knees, Travis adjusted himself to just one. With a single tear running down his face, Travis grabbed Stephanie's hands and said, "We haven't been together for that long and I know this is somewhat out of order. I would have loved to do this the right way by asking your dad first and buying a ring of course. However, Stephanie, knowing you love me and I love you, I need to do what I feel is right in my heart. Stephanie Marie Sinclair, will you do me the honors and become my wife...will you marry me?"

Fanning herself from the tears burning her face, Stephanie let out a tiny squeal and answered with a resounding, "Yes Travis, I'll marry you." Stephanie joked around and said, my nails aren't done anyway so I'm okay with waiting for the ring. Just make sure when you do get the ring, you make it just as special and make sure someone is recording it."

Travis laughed, shook his head, and simply responded, "Yes dear."

Chapter 37

"Good morning, good morning, how's everyone doing on this fine morning." Mother Montgomery asked shuffling into the breakfast nook.

"I'm doing fantastic grandma. I was just telling dad and Cherie about the good news I received about my program. Even better than that, I already have my first enrollee, I meet with him on Monday morning. I'm so happy, this is like a dream come true." Cayden-James said grinning.

Clueless, Cherie said, "So you are supposedly going to help other jailbirds like yourself? What is this program all about again?"

"You ought not be so flip on your lips. You could learn something from him, Cayden-James is doing a remarkable work, I decree and declare, he will change lives and bring people to Christ through his ministry."

Using sarcasm, Cayden-James replied, "I'm not worried about her dad, she's such a huge source of support. For the unlearned, like Cherie my program is called, *The Hedge*, it's play on words, to indicate investments like hedge funds on the natural side but on the spiritual side, it's like we're believing God to put a hedge of protection around them as they reenter into society."

Raising her eyebrows, Cherie said, "I'm impressed, tell me more, I may want to sow into your little jail bird project."

Exhaling a deep breath, Cayden-James continued, "I plan to implement weekly support groups where I start them out paper trading until they learn the basics and fundamentals of trading. At which point they are ready to start trading with money, I will start them off with a $1000.00 bank. I will work with them to build up their portfolios, in an effort to generate income for them and their families. On the other part of the program, they will meet with Ali so she can compile research and build psychological profiles on them. There's more to it but that's the basis."

Mother Montgomery jumped in and said, "I think it all sounds wonderful and speaking of Ali, she seems to be a fine young lady. Are there any more of those delightful little brownie things she and Clarice made?"

Smiling, Cayden-James offered an apology, as he walked past Mother Montgomery, "I'm sorry Grandma but I killed what was left, I had Clarice make them for me this morning. You know what they say, the early bird gets the worm."

Cherie whined about not having the opportunity to taste the brownie breakfast bites.

Bishop laughed and teased Cherie, "Baby girl, I'm here to tell you, you missed a treat."

Giving a once over to her grandson as he tossed his trashed, Mother said, "You talking about you know what they say about that early bird, well I hope you know what they say 'bout men wearing skinny jeans. Can you even breath? I thought you wanted some kids one day, you need to take them off and start over son. Listen to me when I tell you, go put on another pair of pants and burn those."

The family was rolling as Cayden-James tried to figure out what was wrong with his pants.

Cherie chimed in, "She's right, you do need to get rid of those, you are showing all of your business. You never know, you might end up attracting the wrong kind of attention."

Since the breakfast brownies were gone, Clarice brought Mother Montgomery her regular breakfast. Mother looked at Cherie and said, "See, I knew I was right, you just nasty Cherie."

"Why am I nasty? I heard that before, that's like a sign or something they look for. Some men check for other men when they wear those because the packages are easily identifiable."

Cayden-James threw his hands up and said, "That's it, y'all win, I'm going to change and grandma, I will not only burn these but every other pair I have."

The good times continued with the family as they shared jokes and laughs.

Mother poured a stream of Wilson's honey into her morning tea from a plastic bear and said, "Nasty Cherie, tell me something. In any of the times you were with Blue, did you all ever use honey in your shenanigans?"

Sliding down in the chair, Cherie yelled out, "How did this turn to me? I thought we were cracking jokes on Cayden-James, not me."

Bishop's smile went slack, looking at Cherie, he pointed towards his mother and said, "Answer her question."

Using her hair to hide her face, Cherie said, "I'm so embarrassed right now but um, yeah, that was one of Blue's toys of choice, he used to like saying, "honey-dipped" and let me tell you, he could do somethings with that honey."

Shaking his head, Bishop said, "Thanks but You've told us enough. Mother, did you have a particular reason for asking her that?"

Eating her breakfast, Mother Montgomery said, "Mother just asking questions is all son. I have a few for you in fact?"

"Good, now it's your turn." Cherie replied.

"Have you heard anything from Carson and have you heard anything from the private investigator you hired?" Mother asked.

Rocking in place, Bishop responded, "No, I still haven't heard from Carson but I did hear back from the P.I. According to him, he hasn't been able to track him online anywhere. Carson isn't using any credit cards, he emptied out all the cash in his accounts and there aren't any new swipes on his passport. Which means one of two things, either he's still in the country or he has a fake one. His cellphone is still active but they tracked it back to his house. This is the craziest thing to me. My son is wanted in a murder investigation and I can't get in touch with him. Crazy, just crazy."

"Carson don't want to be found. I keep trying to tell y'all that. He's doing the same things he made that poor girl, his first wife, Scarlett do. I tell you what, though, old mother here has a few tricks up her sleeve." Mother continued her breakfast, "Okay, well, moving on from that, I hear you're going out on a date tonight, right?" Mother said smiling.

Jerking back, Cherie exclaimed, "A date? With who?"

Shaking his head in denial, Bishop said, "I'm not going on a date, I'm going to a movie screening."

Giggling, Cherie said, "Is that what you old folks call it these days, "movie screenings?"

Mother Montgomery swatted at Cherie and said, "You are going to get enough of calling people old. You just keep on waking up every day, you'll see what happens." Turning her attention to her son, Mother Montgomery said with a look of approval, "Whatever you're choosing to call it, I'm glad you're going."

Chapter 38

"You beat me here I see; I hope I haven't kept you waiting."

"Not at all, not by much. It's nice to see you again Delores, you look lovely this evening." Bishop complimented.

"Why thank you, you don't look too bad yourself." Delores said joking.

Only she wasn't joking.

After Regina's death, Bishop Montgomery had become less concerned about his appearance. Since he wasn't preaching, he'd ditched the suits and traded them for more casual clothes. Wherein he used to dye his hair to keep a more youthful look, he was now allowing his wisdom and maturity to grow forth. His freshly cut, wavy locks matched his newly trimmed up salt and peppered goatee. Removing his aviator styled sunglasses showcased his new look of dignified distinction. He'd always been an attractive man but tonight, he was handsome and looking from head to toe and Delores was taking note.

As well as the others, he was definitely being checked out.

Walking inside of the building where the pre-screen reception was taking place, Peter Walker, an up and coming filmmaker and guest at the Bolts greeted Delores and Bishop Montgomery.

"Delores, my dear. I'm so glad you made it. Do you see everyone enjoying the fruits of your labor?" Peter said hugging Delores.

"Yes, everything looks lovely Peter, congratulations. I'm glad I could be here tonight." Delores said.

In addition to being a guest at The Bolts, Peter arranged for Delores' winery to provide the food and drink for the cocktail hour leading into the screening.

"I see you found someone to use your extra ticket," Peter said whispering in Delores' ear.

Blushing, she attempted to make an introduction, "Peter, I'd like for you to meet, Bishop C.E. Montgomery, the Senior Pastor of Wondrous Works Tabernacle Fellowship."

Extending his hand, Peter said, "He needs no introduction, I know exactly who this man is. I came in contact with his ministry some years ago, he delivered a life-changing word for me and I've been following his ministry ever since. It is indeed my honor and privilege to have you here tonight."

Returning the handshake, Bishop Montgomery politely said, "It's nice to meet you. To God be the glory, I'm glad you've been blessed."

Delores and Peter continued to talk, Bishop pulled out his phone to check the time. He looked at Peter and Delores and said, "Excuse me for a moment."

Feeling a bit on edge, Bishop went outside where several guests were enjoying themselves, laughing and drinking. He felt like he needed a minute to gain composure but he couldn't understand why. He wanted a glass of wine to calm his nerves but he thought better of it given the public environment he was in.

Admiring the landscape, Bishop turned when he felt fingers crawling up his back, fingers attached to a voice that called out, "Bishop Montgomery."

To his surprise, Mother Montgomery was standing there smiling. "Why are you out here and your beautiful date is inside?" She asked.

Bishop's vocal pitched increased several octaves, "Mother, she's not my date and what are you doing here?"

Mother Montgomery did a little two-step, swaying to the music being played by the band and said, "I keep trying to tell y'all. Mother gets around, you see I'm on the V.I.P. list here."

Hardly able to contain himself, Bishop replied, "Yes, I do see, Ms. V.I.P. Had I known you were coming, I could've driven you." Bishop said.

"No son, I got my own ride here and I'll get my own ride back. I don't want to be depending on nobody to take me anywhere. You will probably be out longer than what I'm planning. I'm going to service in the morning, are you? It's been a while since you last went."

"Yes, I plan to be there Mother. Claude wants me to be there but you know I've been streaming the services; I just haven't felt up to physically going to the sanctuary on Sundays." Bishop replied.

Their mother and son moment was interrupted when Sharon Halston, a former classmate and investor in the film walked up and greeted them.

"Oh my goodness, it has been such a long time. How wonderful it is to see you two. Mrs. Montgomery, you haven't aged a bit." Sharon exclaimed.

Mother turned her nose up and said, "Well thank you dear, the anointing will preserve you."

Stroking the length of her neck and licking her lips, Sharon stepped in closer and said, "C.E. you look like we did in High School, how do you do it. I must know your secrets, you must tell me," she said winking.

Bishop's faced turned a nice shade of crimson which sent his mother looking for the nearest exit. She returned seconds later with Delores and whispered, "This is the third time I've come to you. See, I keep trying to tell you but no, you won't listen. You gone keep right on, you know what they say, three strikes and you're out."

Surveying the playing field, Delores noticed Sharon's particular style of touchy-feely and smiled at Mother Montgomery and said, "Well you know they also say, three times a charm. So, I guess it's all in how you look at it."

Bishop spotted Delores and used her as a way to escape Sharon, although Sharon was not willing to let him go that easily.

Easing up next to Bishop, Delores said, "Well hello there Sharon. It's been a long time, how've you been?"

"Uh-huh, Delores Bolton, it has been a long time." Sharon said.

"I guess it's like an old reunion huh, I see you've gotten reacquainted with my date." Delores said.

Throwing her head back, Sharon gasped, "Your date?"

Bishop heard her as well and thought, "*Her date*?"

Mother walked off chuckling saying, "Her date."

Delores grabbed Bishop by the hand and said, "Yes, my date and I are here to support Peter and from what I understand that includes you, since you are the financier. Congratulations on the film, we look forward to seeing it. Looking at Bishop and then at Sharon, Delores said, "Will you please excuse us, thanks."

Chapter 39

"I'm sure you've heard by now right?"

"Heard what?" Scarlett asked.

James crawled into bed and said, "You haven't talked to your mom?"

"No, I haven't. Chandler was fussy, I was definitely in my feelings, and the baby in here wasn't cooperating either so I turned my phone off so I could get some rest." Scarlett explained.

James realized something.

"Wait a minute, you didn't answer your phone and Minta didn't come over here banging on the door?" James said laughing.

The realization hit Scarlett and she too began to laugh saying, "No, she didn't come over...hmph, now that's different."

Snuggling up next to his wife, James said, "Well, I talked to George and he said Minta found out some real heavy stuff about that girl."

James filled Scarlett in on the recent findings about Amira.

Pouting with her arms folded across her stomach, Scarlett declared, "Well, I don't care if she is crazy, I'm still mad at Travis. I can't believe he'd put us in danger like that."

Rubbing his wife's stomach, James said, "Travis didn't put us in danger, a girl with mental issues did and as it turns out, we're not in danger. Her parents will be here tomorrow to get her. You shouldn't be so hard on him, he's your brother and you need to cut him some slack. At the time, he was new to the family and he was nervous and rightfully so. Hey, it's not easy blending in with the Watson clan. I can't say I blame the man for releasing some stress while on vacation. Just too bad he released in the wrong spot."

Playfully pushing James, Scarlett yelped, "James."

Switching gears, Scarlett asked, "So that crisis seems to be averted, thank God, but what's up with the petition, have you heard anything else?"

James leaned back and said, "I told you, we are rock solid on the adoption. We did everything by the book, we crossed every T and dotted all I's. So we are good on that, the only thing I don't like is having situations like Amira pop up. Especially when we don't know what Carson is capable of. Our lawyers responded to his petition and he hasn't responded. When I was out in California, I hired a private investigator and based on what he told me. He's apparently done what he made you do, it looks like he's disappeared and started a new life."

"Wow, if he was going to do that I wonder why he went through the process of filing a petition?" Scarlett speculated.

"Who knows and who cares, I certainly don't. Carson Montgomery is a moot point in my life...our lives and honestly, I wish him nothing but the best wherever he is." James pronounced.

Thinking back to the day Carson handed her the book, "*How to Disappear and Start a New Life,*" she felt like so much had happened and she was indeed living a new life.

James said, "I guess you hadn't heard about Cole and Marissa either, huh?"

"No, what's going on with them?"

"They're leaving tomorrow."

"To go where?"

James sat up and said, "Cole has done an extended rental at a beach house in Florida somewhere, I think they'll be gone for at least a month, if not longer."

"Can he take that much time, given he just opened his bank?" Scarlett asked.

"I guess you can when you own it." James replied.

Scarlett slid back under the covers and laid on James' bare chest. "In a way, I felt guilty I was still pregnant after they'd lost their baby."

With exaggeration, James criticized, "Why do you do that?"

"Do what?" Scarlett asked.

"How did you make their situation be about you? Why would you even take on that layer of guilt when you know as well as I do, them losing their baby has nothing to do with us still having ours." James shouted.

Looking downward and shaking her head, Scarlett began to cry, "I was only trying to tell you how I felt. I'm sad for them and I feel like I can't be happy for myself too much because I don't want to upset them or make them feel bad."

James consoled Scarlett and said, "I'm sorry. Those are your feelings and I shouldn't have dumped on them. I just don't want you taking on anything you don't need or have to. I think we should put a pin here and try to get some rest."

Kissing Scarlett's hand, James turned off his lamp and cuddled up next to his wife.

Chapter 40

"Carson, where are you son?" Mother Montgomery thought as she sat in front of her computer. Slipping her shoes off from the movie screening, she signed into all of her social media accounts.

Taking a few moments to get dressed for bed, Mother did a little reading in her bible and said prayer, focusing on Mark 4:22, *"Father, God in heaven, You are the creator of the universe, You Father are the creator of everything. We may not know where Carson is but You do. Father, your word declares everything hidden will be brought into the open, eventually and that every secret thing God, will be brought into the light. Lord, we need You to do it. We need you to shine Your light on this situation and reveal to us what we need to know. I thank You Father for it now, I thank You for the manifestation because I believe, I receive, when I pray. In Jesus' name, I pray. Amen."*

Going back over to the computer, Mother Montgomery checked her email and a few messages she had on social media.

A thought crossed her mind and she pondered on it for a while. She looked around online for a few more moments and decided, she'd give her idea a try.

Her fingers graced the keyboard and found one of Carson's profiles, he was previously an active user on social media but he'd closed all of them except one. Mother Montgomery saw this as a sign. There wasn't anything recent on his page but she took a chance and sent him a private message that read:

"Grandma's here for you. You don't have to be afraid. God hasn't given us the spirit of fear, but He's given us power, love, and a sound mind. I don't necessarily need to know where you are but I do need to know you are alright. God loves you and we do too."

Chapter 41

"So what did you think of the movie?"

"I thought it was wonderful. Now it could be because I remember the last time I saw one but I enjoyed it." Bishop said laughing.

Leaning in towards Bishop, Delores replied, "I did too and the company wasn't too bad either."

Bishop's head titled as he gave a slight smile, he was enjoying the playful and lighthearted banter between them, it added a new layer of fun to their interactions. Each time they'd seen it each other it was always so serious and tonight, they happy-go-lucky. The pair decided to go out for coffee after the screening.

"Who knew in High School that Sharon Sinclair would become a big time movie producer and who knew you'd give her some of her old mean girl ways from back in the day?" Bishop asked.

"I was merely letting the lady know what time it was and what time it wasn't." Delores chuckled. "I hope the film does well for them, I know Peter deserves every good thing coming to him."

Fumbling around in her purse, Delores felt the heat from Bishop's eyes, "You're staring at me."

Bishop's voice came down an octave to say, "Yes I am, you are so beautiful and sometimes it's hard for me to take my eyes off of you."

Hearing those words caused her heart to race but she continued with the race to find a special item in her purse.

"I found it." Delores exclaimed.

"Found what?"

"This. Do you remember this?"

Delores held up two tattered tickets tucked in a small plastic case.

Bishop Montgomery grabbed the case out of her hand and said, "You still have these? Do I remember, of course I remember, I just can't believe you kept these after all these years. How could I forget the night we snuck out to the concert of the year? That's also the night I told you I..."

Bishop paused, he didn't want to push his luck and he feared if he continued he would ruin an otherwise perfect evening.

However, Delores finished it for him saying, "That was the night you told me you loved me, right?"

Bishop became unaware of everything and everyone around him, he closed his eyes to savor the experience and feeling he was having. It was a moment he'd thought of over the years but not too much because of Regina. However, Delores was someone he couldn't erase. She'd left an indelible imprint upon his heart.

"That's right," he whispered.

Delores and Bishop Montgomery talked and reminisced about the forbidden concert they went to. Good church folks weren't supposed to be going to hear the devil's music but these two gave way to the temptation and partied until they couldn't party any more. To them, the risk of getting caught was worth it, luckily they didn't.

Bishop looked long at Delores and suggested a future meeting, a near future one, "Would you mind being my guest at church tomorrow? I'll understand if you can't or don't want to."

Delores smiled and said, "I accept, I'd love to. Is there anything I need to know in particular?"

"Nope, all I need you to do is show up and I'll take care of the rest."

Wishing he could stay and talk with her all night, Bishop knew the right thing to do was end the evening on a bright note. He stood up tossed their empty trash. Holding out his hand, he said, "My lady, may I walk you to your car?"

Bishop Montgomery was always protective of her, even back when they were together. He was the chivalrous type and still was. He opened the door for her and waited until she was safely buckled in her seat. With her window down, he said, "Text me when you get home and let me know you made it there safely."

"I will, you drive safely too and I'll see you in the morning." Delores said as she backed out.

Bishop stood on the sidewalk and watched her leave, he placed his hand over his heart and tapped it several times before he walked to his car.

Chapter 42

"Look out now, my dad is first day of school sharp today. Whoa man, I haven't seen you dress like this in months, what do you have going on today? I thought Uncle Claude was speaking today, did something change?"

"No C.J., I'm just looking forward to service today." Bishop eluded. "Are you riding with me or do you have other plans?"

Checking his phone, Cayden-James asked, "How long before you leave? Ali is on her way out here, if you can wait a few minutes, yeah, we'll ride with you."

"Things going well for you two, huh?" Bishop asked.

"Very well." Cayden-James shouted.

Walking towards his son, Bishop Montgomery placed his hand on Cayden-James' shoulders and said, "Son, you have no idea how that makes me feel to hear you say that. We talked about her not too long ago and now look. I want you to know I think she's a fine young lady. You also need to know you deserve to be happy, don't let nothing or no one tell you otherwise. The Lord has many good things in store for you and I want you, my boy to pursue them all with perseverance. Always persevere my boy, persevere."

Cayden-James grabbed his father and hugged him saying, "Thanks dad, it means a lot to hear you say that and I will, I promise, I'll keep at it and never give up."

Bishop smiled and said, "That's my boy."

Mother Montgomery walked by the two on her way to the family room saying, "Two of my favorite men. You both look very nice this morning."

Inside the family room, Cherie was sprawled out on the sofa, under a blanket, and in her pajamas.

"Another Sunday here at the house?" Mother Montgomery asked as she put on her pearl earrings.

"Yep, you got a problem with that? I'm sure you do." Cherie said with a roll of the eyes.

Mother grabbed her things and said, "Hey, it's your soul, not mine. The bible tells us to work out our own salvation with fear and trembling, we all have different interpretations of that. You do it your way and I'll keep on doing it the way I know how. Alright now, grandma will see you after church. I hope you will look a different when we get back for brunch."

Rolling over onto her side, turning her back towards Mother Montgomery, pulling the blanket over her head, Cherie said, "We'll see."

Mother Montgomery stood over her and said, "I'm gone say a special prayer for you."

Standing all together in the foyer, Ali, Cayden-James, and Bishop Montgomery, all smiled when Mother Montgomery walked out towards them. The driver was outside waiting to transport them to the sanctuary.

Driving onto the church's grounds, Delores was stopped at the entrance by one of the parking lot attendants. Surprised, Delores put her window down. "Excuse me ma'am. Good morning, we are delighted to have you with us. I've been instructed to have you pull your car over. If you wouldn't mind, I'm going to need you to get out and hand me your keys. I promise, you'll get them back."

With hesitation, Delores said, "I've been to this church a million times, this has never happened to me before. What is going on here?"

Pulling up next to her car, a gorgeous young lady jumped out of a golf cart and said, "Good morning Ms. Delores, we are so happy to have you with us today at Wondrous Works, I'm Natalie Smalls and I'll be taking care of you today." Natalie, a member of the amour bearer team at the church stepped back to have the attendant open Delores' door and said, "Will you please follow me, it will be my pleasure to escort you to the sanctuary."

Delores stalled a bit before grabbing her things, she asked a question for clarification, "Are you all doing this because Bishop Montgomery told you I was coming?"

The attendant responded, "Yes ma'am, he waiting for you inside."

Handing over her keys, Delores walked over and got in the front seat of the cart.

Natalie accompanied Delores to Bishop's office, making small talk along the way.

Bishop sat listening to music at his desk, his entire countenance brightened when Natalie brought Delores in to greet him. Natalie excused herself and informed Delores she'd be waiting for her outside the door.

Standing, Bishop held out his hand for Delores, "Good morning, I'm so glad to have you here. You look beautiful."

Still somewhat shocked, Delores said, "Really, did it require all of that? A full production to get me in here, I would have been just fine walking through the front door like everyone else."

Shaking his head, Bishop Montgomery said, "Oh no no, you are a special guest of mine and it is our pleasure to treat you as such. If you think that's too much, you should see what we do for our first time visitors."

Delores laughed so hard and Bishop followed suit, their communal humor sliced through any lingering anxieties they were experiencing.

Bishop Montgomery gave more details as to how the morning was going to proceed. "I hope you don't embarrass easily. I'm not going to put you on the spot but I am going to acknowledge you. I will be on the stage of course but you will be seated on the front row, Natalie will be behind you in case you need anything. You will be seated next to Ali, my son's girlfriend and a few others."

Taking in all of the information, Delores swallowed hard and said, "Okay, I think I got it."

"Now that I have you here, I hope you know this means you have to join us for brunch afterwards." Bishop said.

"Brunch? What kind of brunch are you talking about here?" Delores said slowly.

With a huge grin, Bishop said, "My family and I have brunch after church every Sunday back at my house and all guests of mine have to attend."

Bishop Montgomery threw that last part in there but only because he didn't want his day to end so soon with Delores.

"You think your family will be fine with that?"

"I don't see why not?"

Delores fidgeted around with the ring on her finger and said, "Okay, why not? I'd love to."

Bishop was about to lean in for a hug when Natalie tapped on the door, "Excuse me Bishop but it's time and I'd like to get Ms. Delores seated."

"Sure thing Natalie." Bishop said smiling. "I'll see you out there, okay Delores?"

Walking out of the office with a new pep in her step, Delores turned back waving and said, "If I don't see you first."

Chapter 43

"Oh my goodness, we can't thank you enough for calling us about our daughter. It's been a hard couple of weeks. Julian's call to us was an answer to our prayers."

"Well, I'm sure you can imagine our surprise when we found out about your daughter's situation and that she was here with us. Minta replied.

Nadine and Joel Rosier arrived in Jordan to be reunited with their daughter, Amira. They hugged and thanked the Watsons repeatedly.

Travis wiped his forehead as beads of sweat pooled around his hairline.

Amira's mother revealed to the Watsons, "I'm not sure whether my drug use or our strict parenting is what sent Amira over the edge. She started displaying signs as a young girl and as she got older, her symptoms worsened."

Minta handed Nadine a handkerchief and said, "How bad is it because from what we witnessed, I'm wondering why isn't she institutionalized?"

Nadine nodded and said, "She has been. We were trying out something different though. As long as she takes her meds, she's fine and she was being consistent in taking her medicine. As a result, they allowed her to come home, the condition would be to remain on the medicine. Apparently something caused her to relapse. I'm just so thankful our MiMi is alright."

The families stood in the parking lot of Travis' apartment. They were waiting for Dr. Middleton to arrive. Unsure of how Amira would respond to an ambush, a well-meaning one but ambush none the less, Minta didn't want to take any chances.

The families went over the game plan once again, making sure everyone knew how things were going to go. With their careful planning, the extraction was set to go on without a hitch.

The families walked up the stairs to Travis' floor. Nadine, Joel, George, Minta, and Dr. Middleton stayed back, down the hall as Travis knocked on the door.

No one answered.

He knocked again. Still no answer.

Checking the door knob, the door was unlocked. He took his time to open it.

Peaking around the door, Travis walked in slowly calling out, "Amira, I'm here." He'd made a call to her earlier to let her know the family had made a decision and he'd bring over what she wanted.

The apartment was empty, Amira wasn't there.

Running down the hallway, Travis said breathing heavy, "She's not in there."

Amira's parents began to cry, "You told us our daughter was here," they yelled.

Minta encouraged Travis to call her.

George huddled everyone together and said, "We should probably go inside."

Waiting for an answer, Travis said, "Hey girl, I'm here at the apartment, where are you? I thought you said you would be here waiting."

"Hey Travis, since today is going to be our last day together, I thought we could have breakfast one last time, kind of like how we did on the island. You sound nervous, I only walked down the street to this little bagel shop. I'll be there in a few minutes."

"I was nervous because you left the front door unlocked but okay, I'll be here waiting." Travis hung up the phone and ran in the apartment speaking in a high-pitched, high-speed voice, "She's down the street, we need a new plan. You guys need to hang out in one of the bed rooms until she gets comfortable. No one needs to come out until...we need some sort of code word."

Minta walked over to Travis and said, "Calm down son, we will listen closely and figure out when the best time to come out is." Making a joke, Minta said, "Do me a favor and make sure she doesn't have any sharp objects in her hands."

Travis smiled and said, "Oh my God, I'm so nervous, I can barely breath."

"Take in a deep cleansing breath. Don't worry, this will all be over soon. You can then put this behind you and move on with our dear, sweet Stephanie. I'm so happy for you two Travis. We need to go ring shopping though." Minta cheered.

George cleared his throat and said, "I think it's time to get into place."

Within minutes, Amira arrived with a brown paper bag and a drink holder. "Well hello Travis, aren't you going to help me, you see I'm struggling to get in the door with all of this stuff in my hands."

Jumping up, Travis said, "Oh, I'm sorry Amira, I wasn't thinking. So what all do you have here?"

Watching Amira remove the breakfast from the bags, Travis kept a careful eye on her and the doors to the back bedrooms.

Amira erupted into a laughing frenzy and said, "I probably went overboard, I practically brought up everything in the store. You can do that when you're about to hit the jack pot, right Travis?"

Reaching for the last item, Amira motioned for Travis to have a seat, he made sure to sit on the bar stool closest to the kitchen.

"You know Travis, I just want you to know, none of this was personal so don't beat yourself up to bad about it okay." Amira said.

Raising his voice, Travis said, "I'm not planning to beat myself up, I've made peace with it. I don't know how much peace you'll have though, MiMi."

Upon hearing Travis' last words, Amira stood unnaturally still. At a snail's pace, Amira's coffee cup left her mouth and found its way to the countertop. She fixed her eyes on Travis and said, "What did you just say?"

The hair on the nape of Travis' neck raised up, his legs tightened as he angled his body to make a run for it.

At the same time, both Amira and Travis' eyes landed on the knife block, he forgot to move at Minta's suggestion.

Backing away, Travis raised his voice again, "Uh, hello, now would be a good time..."

As he was speaking, Nadine rushed out and called out to Amira, "MiMi, oh MiMi, mom's here."

One by one, everyone came out from the bedrooms.

Seeing her parents, Amira reached for the knives, grabbing one, she held it up to herself and looked at her parents, smiled and said, "MiMi's dead."

Minta and Nadine screamed aloud and what sounded like in slow motion, "No."

Seconds before lodging a serrated knife into her stomach, George knocked her over from behind. Travis grabbed the knife and her father assisted George on the ground. The two men held her down long enough for Dr. Middleton to administer a sedative.

Chapter 44

The praise and worship inside of Wondrous Works uplifting and heartfelt. From the praise and worship leaders to the band to the singers to the congregation, mouths were opened, hands were clapping, feet were tapping and bodies were swaying.

The Sunday morning medley had everyone on their feet, the songs from the old church fired up the members and as they sang songs and melodies unto the Lord.

Mother Montgomery looked down her row in an attempt to catch Delores attention.

Breaking her time of praise, Delores looked around to identify the source of eyes she felt staring at her. There she spotted Mother Montgomery, clapping her hands with a nod in her direction. It was a nod loaded with approval, an endorsement of her being there and her attire.

Given the fact, Delores hadn't been briefed on the attire, she dressed as if she knew all of the particulars. Based on Mother's nod, she'd nailed it.

After the jubilant time, Bishop Montgomery was called to the podium to greet the congregation. He received a standing ovation as he approached.

Standing there with his fist over his heart, Bishop Montgomery received the love from his parishioners all over the building. Thunderous applause and cheers were heard all around. Motioning for everyone to take their seats, he said, "I get the impression, you guys love your pastor."

The church erupted again as they crowd stood to express their love and appreciation.

"Man, do I love Wondrous Works Tabernacle Fellowship. I greet you all in the name of our Father, I'm so blessed to be here this morning. I want you all to know I appreciate your prayers and I don't want them to stop, keep praying for your pastor. Will you all do that for me? If you will do that for me, say amen."

The jam-packed audience chimed in together saying, "Amen."

"Well alright, that is wonderful. I want to give honor to my lovely mother, Mother Montgomery. Can you all give her a hand? Doesn't she look beautiful today?"

Mother Montgomery stood up and waved to the crowd, before taking her seat, she blew a kiss towards the stage.

"I'd also like to recognize my son, Cayden-James, he's up here on the platform with us. Come on over her son." Bishop instructed.

As Cayden-James made his way over, Bishop said, "As he's on his way, let's give a hand to his significant other, Ali, she's in the audience there. Ali, stand up and let the people see you."

Ali followed Mother's movements, waving and sitting down.

"Hey church, this is my baby boy here, he's no longer a baby though. He's grown into a fine young man, one I look up to and highly respect. He's faithful and an inspiration to all who know him. He has a new program that I'm so excited about. The church is partnering with him and he will get some time to share his vision towards the end of the service. My brother, Pastor Claude has been gracious to fill in for us and we appreciate him but I just wanted my son to join me for a minute so you all can see the future of our church."

The members clapped and cheered as if to say they were in agreement with Bishop's words. Ali's heart swelled with pride.

Cayden-James turned and walked back to his seat. Which means there was one other person left for Bishop to introduce. Delores knew her turn was coming. She attempted to smooth out her suit and straighten any puckers in her pantyhose.

"Before I take my seat, I am honored to have my friend from High School, a former member and employee of Wondrous Works here with me today. Will you all please welcome Delores Bolton back home?" Bishop announced.

Standing from the stage, Bishop's face glowed looking at Delores. From the way he introduced her to the way he looked at her and the smile that radiated from her looking at him, they were sending messages. It wasn't necessarily what he said but his mannerisms signified to those interested parties...Delores was the new lady in his life.

Taking his seat, Bishop Montgomery glanced again in Delores direction and established eye contact with her. They both shared a shy-like smile.

Claude took his cue and said, "Let's give Bishop Montgomery another hand, my brother, we are glad to have you here with us today."

Dressed in his preaching robe, Claude did his own set of greetings, honoring his wife, Lillian and their family. He honored Mother Montgomery a second time. She didn't mind, she took it all in.

Claude began his message by saying, "I love this church, this church is in my DNA, I am a product of Wondrous Works and I'm humbled by the opportunity to stand behind this sacred desk and preach the word of God. I want you to know I intend to be very transparent with you today. The lord has given me a message, specific to this house, to this body of believers and I pray you are ready to receive.

Taking a sip of water, Claude said, "This church has been in my family for generations and I have to say, I'm proud of that fact. You know, growing up I envisioned I would be the senior pastor of this church but as it turns out, my dad, made the decision to grant my brother the position. Can I be honest with you? I was mad. I was hurt. I was angry. So angry, I chose to leave my family here at Wondrous Works and I lost all connections and ties with my family. I told them to go to, well you all know where I told them to go. I told them to leave me alone and to never try and contact me. Oh yeah, I made sure they knew how angry I was. I showed them, right? Wrong. For years and years, I missed them and I wanted to reach out but my stupid pride wouldn't allow me to."

The atmosphere inside the church was tight, everyone was clinging to each word spoken by Claude.

Moving about the stage, Claude resumed, "Have any of you been wondering why I was so angry I didn't get the church? I mean, he was the eldest son, one would think he should've gotten it. Well, in my mind, I worked harder than him. I shed blood, sweat, and tears for this ministry, wherein, all my brother did was sit around and look pretty."

Everyone roared with laughter, Claude laughed and said, "I'm just kidding, he did more than that. He walked around and looked pretty." The laughs continued.

"Seriously though, I felt like if I worked hard enough for the church, for sure, my father would grant me the charge to lead the church. Here is where I begin my message, I thought by doing everything right, by attempting to uphold every single commandment, I would be the perfect candidate. Romans 3:20 says, "Therefore no one will be declared righteous in God's sight by the works of the law; rather, through the law we become conscious of our sin. Now don't get me wrong, works are important because, in the previous chapter, Paul says in chapter two that God will render to each one according to his works." Claude explained.

The congregation tuned their hearts and their ears towards Claude, they were completely plugged into his message.

Keeping on with his point, Claude said, "When I left here, I was finishing my studies as a political science major but I was determined to start my own church. I had to show my family I didn't need to be the pastor at Wondrous Works, I could be my own pastor at my own church. Are you all following me when I say I had to show them what the real deal was? I needed to show my father he'd made a mistake; he'd named the wrong son. In the meantime, I started working on a local political campaign, straight out of college, I was the lowest one on the totem but I was a pastor. As it turns out, the candidate I worked with won. I began to work on more campaigns and guess what, the candidates won."

Laying the foundation for his sermon, Claude walked back to the podium and said, "For years, with the help of the Lord, the church did grow and flourish but so did my political career. I hope you all are beginning to the see the parallel here. I was *working* hard for the ministry but I was being *graced* for the ministry of politics. There were times I turned down political opportunities because I had a church to run."

Wiping the corners of his mouth, Claude said, "I know, I know, I can hear your thoughts. Some of you are sitting here thinking, but Pastor Claude, what about the scripture that says, faith without works is dead, am I right7?"

Many of the members nodded their heads in agreement, he was correct in his assessment.

Claude pointed out something, "This is why you can't build doctrine off of one scripture. People are quick to say the bible seems to contradict itself but let me tell you, our God is not the author of confusion. It would appear that James and Paul are in conflict with their words about works but in order to understand they are preaching the same thing; you need to understand the context."

Flipping through his notes, Claude said, "Ephesians 2:8-9 states, I like reading it out of the Amplified, it says:

> 8 For it is by grace [**God's remarkable compassion and favor drawing you to Christ**] that you have been saved [**actually delivered from judgment and given eternal life**] through faith. And this [**salvation**] is not of yourselves [**not through your own effort**], but it is the [**undeserved, gracious**] gift of God; 9 not as a result of [**your**] works [**nor your attempts to keep the Law**], so that no one will [**be able to**] boast *or* take credit in any way [**for his salvation**].

Standing on the edge of the stage, Claude spoke up and said, "I want you to envision something for me. Imagine if you will, a conveyor belt, it's a carrier medium, mostly there are items being moved along the way in a particular direction.

---

7 **James 2:17:** *"Even so faith, if it hath not works, is dead, being alone."* **(KJV)**

Instead of seeing items on the belt, I want you to place, works and grace on it. In one direction, this was the direction I was moving in, I was working towards Christ, I was working to maintain my salvation. Yes, I was preaching and teaching grace and about the finished work of the cross but I had not yet fully accepted and received God's grace for my life."

Picking up the pace, Claude said, "Listen folks, salvation is an exchange, we should hit the reverse button on our conveyor belt. The saving grace of faith comes when we stop putting our trust in the works we do and replace that with the works of Jesus, the finished work of the cross. When we replace the trust in ourselves with the trust in Christ, the faith in our lives will begin to produce good works. Do you all see the difference?"

Several people were standing and clapping, nodding their heads as they began to understand.

"I promise if you all stick with me for a little longer, I have something to say," Claude announced. "Some time back, I was praying and meditating and the Lord dropped Joshua 18:3[8] in my spirit and when I tell you, it was like He was asking me that question. You see, Joshua, the right hand man to Moses was chosen to lead the people into the promised land after his beloved leader had passed. Joshua and the tribes were supposed to go and conquer Canaan, they were supposed to live there and develop the land, their promised land had squatters and they were supposed to go in and drive them out. Problem was, some of the tribes were dragging their feet, they weren't doing the necessary things to possess the land they'd

---

[8] **Joshua 18:3:** *"Joshua asked them, "How long are you going to wait before taking possession of the remaining land the LORD, the God of your ancestors, has given to you?"* (**NIV**)

been given. Joshua called a come to Jesus moment and asked them point blank. I need to draw a parallel, the same way Joshua asked those tribes, God was asking me, how long are you going to wait before taking possession of the land I've given you? You see, the Lord had given me the land of politics to conquer. How many of you agree we need some believers in politics? Yeah, I agree. I yielded myself to Him that day and I agreed to go in and take over my promised land."

People all over the church were on their feet. Claude instructed them to sit down, "Hold on, I have a bit more to say, take your seats for just a few more minutes. This is about to get really good."

Going in for the close, Claude said, "Shortly after that day, I heard the horrible news about my sister-in-law's tragic accident. I reached out to brother in his time of need and God allowed restoration to take place in my family as evidenced by me standing here today. Years I'd lost had been returned just like that. I was honored and humbled by his request to have me fill in for him. You all know the story but what you don't know is that today is my last Sunday preaching here at Wondrous Works."

The crowd was taken by surprise.

"I have to say, I didn't know my brother was going to bring my nephew up here today but let me show you how prophetic it was. I'm talking about Joshua and how after Moses died, he led the people into their promised land. Well, as my brother said earlier, my nephew is the future of this church, I believe he will be a symbol of the Joshua generation that will take Wondrous Works far into the future." Claude shouted.

Both Cayden-James and Ali's mouth dropped open.

Claude motioned for Bishop and Cayden-James to come stand with him on the stage.

Wiping his face, Claude smiled and said. "As I stand here with these mighty men of God, I'm here to officially announce I will be running for a seat in the State House, representing district 9. I sure hope I can count on you all for a vote? It has been my pleasure to serve you all here as interim pastor but it is now time for me to possess the land the Lord has given me. It's time for you all to go and possess the lands God has given you. Don't let Him have to ask you how long. Let's do it, let's go and change the world. I love you all."

Chapter 45

"Oh my Lord, that was some crazy and I mean crazy stuff we witnessed earlier. I still can't believe it."

"Travis, I'm just glad she's gone and on a plane back to where she came from and will get the help she needs." Minta said.

After the incident with Amira, Minta decided the family needed to get together and not necessarily celebrate but have a good time and decompress. With several things going on within her family, the get together turned into an impromptu engagement for Travis and Stephanie and a going away party for Cole and Marissa.

The family fellowship was a welcomed distraction to everything going on. The time together was precious. Chandler splashed around with James in the pool as Scarlett sat on the pool's edge tossing in toys. Travis and Stephanie played around in the pool while Cole and Marissa took in some sun. Derek, Rena, George, and Minta worked together to prepare the food for everyone.

Calling everyone inside, Minta said, "I have something I'd like to say, we've been through a lot but in our trials, we've gone through together. There is nothing more important than family. We've all been on a roller coaster of emotions but through it all, God is good and I thank Him for everything, the good, the bad, and the ugly. I believe we are stronger as a family and as long as we stay focused on that, there is nothing we won't be able to handle."

George stepped in and said, "You know, Minta is exactly right. With everything going on, I haven't had a chance to do this. As you all know, one of the last times we were together, out of anger, I said somethings I regret." Laying his hand against his breastbone, George said, "I've apologized to Minta but I need to one, apologize to you guys and two, publicly apologize to my wife. You all have seen me at some of my best moments and definitely some of my worst. That day was one of my worst and I ask you all to forgive me. Minta, I'm sorry and know that I love you very much."

In the spirit of making amends, all of the men looked at their lady loves and declared their love.

With tears, Minta and George kissed and officially made up in front of their family.

Minta spoke up and said, "I have one more thing to say before we eat. We are so excited about Travis and Stephanie's engagement and the life they are going to build together. That new life is already starting off to a great start because the Rosier's were offering a cash reward for information leading to the daughter and the handed me a check this morning. I started not to take it but I decided I would bless these two love birds with it. I want you all to go, build a beautiful life and have plenty of babies."

Caught up in the moment, Minta didn't realize the potential impact her words could have. Marissa shifted in her seat and Minta noticed saying, "Oh honey, I'm sorry."

Shaking her head, Marissa said, "There's no need to be sorry. I agree with you; I want the same things for them. Congratulations Travis and Stephanie."

Cole wrapped his arm around Marissa's waist and kissed her on the cheek.

Trying to fade away, Minta whispered, "Let's eat."

Chapter 46

"I was blessed by your message today son, I'm so glad to have you back with us."

"Thank you Mother, it's good to be back." Claude replied.

Claude's wife Lillian chimed in and said, "Honey, you did so good today. You made me so proud."

Looking down the table, Mother asked, "And how did you enjoy the service today Delores?"

Delores took a moment to respond, her thoughts were all over the place as she was having a hard time processing the fact she was at the traditional after church brunch as Bishop's guest in his house, seated right next to him. In her head, she made sure the sentence made sense before speaking.

Nodding she said, "I too was blessed by the message as I believe it is time for me to take possession of my promise land."

Picking up on the reference, Mother Montgomery smiled and said, "I agree."

Preparing to eat, Mother Montgomery said, C.E. when you bless the food, can you please pray for Mother Parrish? Bless her heart, she made a huge mistake. She went to put eye drops in her eyes and mistakenly used super glue. I think she's going to be alright but she might end up with sticky eyes."

Everyone at the table tried not to laugh but it didn't work.

Right before Bishop was about to bless the food, Cherie dilly-dallied her way to an empty seat at the table, one in front of Delores.

Taking her time to sit down, Mother scoffed, "Look what the cat drug in, glad you could join us."

"Isn't this what you wanted? You said you wanted me to be up and ready for brunch, so I'm here." Cherie said with a flip of her lips.

After the blessing, Clarice began to serve and bring out the stainless steel serving dishes. Every time she walked by Delores she said, "Hmph."

Cherie picked up on it and said, "I feel the same way Clarice, I'm not sure my auntiemama would approve. Who is this woman anyway?"

"Watch it Cherie." Mother scolded.

In a way only Bishop could, he looked at Cherie and said, "This woman is a guest in our home, my guest and you will treat her as such. If anyone in here has a problem with that, you can leave."

From the time of Regina's passing, the Montgomery family had experienced the many stages of grief. Based on the makeup of those at the table for Sunday brunch, it appeared they were now in the phase of readjusting with new relationships, new patterns, and renewed hope.

Claude attempted to lift the spirit in the room when he said, "What do you call a preacher and a politician...crazy. That's about all I can come up with but you know what, I think I have a real shot at winning this thing."

It worked. Everyone around the table laughed. Conversations around the table resumed.

Leaning towards Delores, Bishop asked, "Are you okay? Do you want anything else?"

Delores chuckled and said, "I'm fine, I could use a nap since I was on the phone all night like teenagers talking to you."

Bishop smiled and said, "That was fun, huh? I seriously cannot remember the last time I stayed up all night talking to someone." Taking a bite to eat, he leaned over and said, "There's plenty of room here, you know you can take a rest if you want."

"Or I could go home and rest." Delores said sharply.

"But if you did that, you wouldn't be able to spend your Sunday afternoon with me. Now would you?" Bishop said blushing.

Returning the blush, Delores said softly, "No, I wouldn't."

On the other side of the table, Ali said under her breath, "Are you really going to take over the church?"

Shaking his head almost uncontrollably, Cayden-James said, "Oh my God, I had no idea they were going to do that. I was just as surprised as everyone else. I mean, I don't know what the future holds but if that's the path God has for me then we shall see."

"I hear you, switching gears, how are you feeling about seeing your dad with Delores?" Ali asked.

Taking a minute to finish chewing, Cayden-James sat back and said, "You know what, he looks happy. I haven't seen him look happy in a long time and if she makes him look like that, then that makes me happy."

Clearing her plate out of the way, Mother made an announcement, "So as most of you know, the luncheon is this Saturday and I hope all of you ladies will be there. Delores, dear, I hope you will be able to join us."

Unsure of how to respond, Delores just said, "Yes ma'am."

"Good, I look forward to seeing you. Now, Mother is going to go and lay these tired bones down, I have some business to take care of later."

One by one, after Mother Montgomery excused herself, others began to do the same. Claude and his family decided to head out, Claude was scheduled for an appearance for his campaign. Ali and Cayden-James left the dining room as well. Within minutes, the only two remaining were Bishop and Delores.

Grabbing Delores' hand, Bishop said, "You have no idea how happy I was to see you this morning. When Natalie brought you into my office, you took my breath away."

"Ahh, thank you. I was happy to see you too." Delores replied.

"You know I was serious about you taking a nap here, I can have one of the rooms prepared for you." Bishop offered.

"No, no, no, please don't go through that trouble. I'm going to go home and go to sleep in my own bed." Delores said.

Dropping his shoulders, Bishop said, "Okay, if you must. No really, I understand."

"But." Delores said with a smile. "I do have something I want to run by you. I need to make a quick trip back to my house, for like a day or two. I was wondering if you'd like to

come along with me? To help me with the driving of course."
She said laughing.

Whooping it up, Bishop replied, "Road trip." Having a
great time with Delores, he said, "It would be my pleasure to
share driving with you."

Chapter 47

"Are you nervous at all?"

"A little, but I think I'm more excited than nervous, if that makes sense." Cayden-James said.

Picking at her nails, Ali said, "Well, I'm nervous."

"Maybe this will calm you down." Pulling Ali in close to him, Cayden-James moved in and kissed Ali in a deep and sensual way.

With her eyes still closed, Ali said, "I thought the idea was to calm my nerves not rev me up."

Arranging the documents on the table, Cayden-James smiled and said, "The question is, do you feel better?"

Laughing, Ali admitted, "Indeed I do. Now I know where to go whenever I'm nervous."

The couple's play time was over when the visitor they were expecting arrived at Cayden-James' office.

"Uh, yes, good morning, I'm Ronald Douglas and I'm here to see Cayden-James Montgomery."

Ronald Douglas II stood in the doorway of Cayden-James's office, nearly filling up the frame. His broad shoulder's came close to spanning the distance across the door frame. His modest apparel did not match the million dollar smile he wore.

"It's a pleasure to meet you man. I'm Cayden-James and this here is Ali and we're glad to have you here. Come on in and have a seat. We are all ready for you. We have a light breakfast prepared over there if you want anything."

Ronald walked in and looked around the office. Readjusting to the outside world was proving to be somewhat of a challenge for him. Everything about the world had changed.

Cayden-James started off by saying, "So man, I want to start off with you telling me a little about yourself. I know what I've read in your file but I want to hear from you first."

Peeling back the skin from a banana, Ronald said, "Yeah man, well you know how it is. Trying to provide for my family, I got caught up in the wrong game. I got locked up 'bout twenty years ago for slanging. Back in my day, I moved major weight, I was a real kingpin"

Ali and Cayden-James looked at each and then back at Ronald. They had no clue as to what he was referring.

A flush crept over Ronald's face, he shook his head and broke it down, "Let's just say I sold a lot of drugs and I was good at it." Pausing for a minute, he then said, "Well, I was good at it until I got caught."

"Ronald, do you mind me asking, what did you do prior to selling drugs?" Ali asked.

"I was waiting to be picked up by a professional basketball team. I was attending a bunch of training camps and then I got a call my dad needed surgery. I didn't have the amount needed and I started looking for a way to make it happen. I made the money and then because it came so easy, I made a deal with the devil and the rest is history."

"And how did you end up here at the Hedge? I know Warden Peterson referred you but you had a choice in whether or not you'd show up." Ali said.

"That's true and I did mull over whether or not I should come but when I thought about it, I realized, I don't ever want to go back to prison and if this can keep me from going back and get me on my feet, I figure, why not." Ronald exclaimed.

Cayden-James sat up and said, "Well Ronald, it all depends on your level of motivation but I promise, if you give this all you have and commit to the process, you will have more than enough to get on your feet. One thing about and two things for sure, a hustle is a hustle and if you were good at, as you call it, moving major weight, let's transfer that and makes some moves investing. Let's become the kingpins of the stock market. What do you say, are you in?"

Biting off a piece of a muffin, Ronald extended his hand and said, "Let's do this, I'm all in, kingpin."

Chapter 48

"Crazy couple of weeks huh?"

"Oh my word, we've been through a whirlwind here recently." George responded.

"The house seems so empty now with everyone gone but hey, I have something I'd like for us to do. Are you up for it?" Minta asked.

George smiled and said, "Sure, what is it?"

"Give me one second." Minta said holding up one finger.

Minutes later Minta walked into the breakfast area and plopped down a large plastic bag. Inside was a beautiful keepsake box she'd ordered with pictures from their wedding day embossed on the outside. Also inside the bag was card stock, colored pencils, all sorts of arts and crafts, and magazines.

Massaging George's shoulders, Minta stood over him and said, "I have a project for us. I'd like for us to create an aspiration box. This box will serve as things we want to do as a couple, things you and I will aspire to do together. As you can see, I've already started with the box. I found it online, do you like it?"

"I love it, I love the idea, and I love you." George said.

"Perfect. Well, the first thing I want us to do is write each other a handwritten note, expressing what we hope to get out of this exercise. Let's only take five minutes to write it and whatever we have at the end of the timer is what we have. Agreed?" Minta instructed.

George set the timer on his phone and he and Minta went crazy writing their love notes. When the alarm rang, George passed his note over to Minta and she handed him her note. Reading each other's notes, they both laughed so hard. Minta laughed so hard, she snorted. George's laughter turned into tears. George and Minta were already off to a great start of reconnecting and having fun.

Gathering herself together, Minta asked, "How many things should we start off with for our box. The idea is to create the list and then as we check them off, we add another one."

George thought about and said, "Well, if that's the case, let's start with ten items, ranging from small to large aspirations."

Minta reached over for a pen and asked, "How should we do this? Do you want to give an aspiration and I give one and go back and forth or how should we do it?"

With love in his eyes that traveled from his heart, George said, "Well my dear, what do you aspire for us to do together as a couple?"

Tapping the pen at the corner of her mouth, she responded with, "I'd love for us to bless someone with a new car."

George's head jerked back, "Whoa, I thought we were going to start off small? You know how to go right in for it don't you?" George said laughing. "I'm okay with that so let's put it on the list."

Writing the first aspiration down, Minta said, "What's something you'd like for us to do George?"

"Since you started out with a big one, I'm going to keep that spirit alive. I have a two-part aspiration; I hope that's okay? I say let's learn a new language and then go to that country and test out our skills. What do you think?" George asked.

Minta clasped her hands together and said, "Oh George, I love it. What language should we take up? Spanish, French, Portuguese, which one?"

"That's it, I say let's learn some Portuguese and then head off to Rio de Janeiro, I hear it's a beautiful city. I would love to see the Christ the Redeemer statute there." George said.

"Me too, I've always wanted to see that." Minta said writing down George's two-part goals.

Running her fingers up George's arm, Minta flashed a slick smile and said, "You know, we've never made love on a beach. Maybe we can make Brazil a three-part goal. You know they have nude beaches there?"

George slammed his hand on the table and shouted, "Add it. For those three reasons alone, I aspire to go to Brazil with my beautiful wife."

"And I aspire to grow old together with you George Watson." Minta declared.

For the rest of the evening, Minta and George tossed around ideas and aspirations. The exercise allowed them the opportunity to breakthrough any lingering issues they had. Even after nearly thirty years of marriage, they discovered new things about each other. They were able to create new ideas for date nights and they heard new dreams and desires. The project opened them up to strengthening their marriage all while having fun.

Their combined list read as follows:

- Read the same book

- Have a pillow fight
- Bless someone with a car
- Learn a new language - Portuguese
  - Travel to Brazil
  - Make love on the beach
- Create a new board game
- Go on more dates
- Volunteer at the shelter
- Binge watch a new series
- Take Chandler to Disney
- Plant a vegetable garden

Chapter 49

"Good morning my love, how'd you sleep?"

Rolling over, Rebekkah turned towards Godfrey and said, "Good morning, I had some of the best sleep ever. Falling asleep to crashing waves is like a baby's lullaby to me. This beach house is amazing, I'm so glad you chose for us to come to Florida."

Smiling Godfrey asked, "So I did good huh?"

Nuzzling up next to Godfrey, Rebekkah said, "You did better than good, you did great, everything is perfect."

"Well, when I was thinking about where to go, I remembered you said you'd never been to Florida and since this was supposed to be a relaxing vacation, I figured, why not try a beach get-a-way...so here we are and I've been enjoying every minute of it." Godfrey exclaimed.

Standing to go to the bathroom, Rebekkah's robe blew open from the sea breeze which exposed the roundness of her stomach. Noticing, Godfrey laid back and began to reflect. Feeling a heaviness come upon him, he tried to shake it off, he shook his hands in an effort to release negative energy through his fingertips.

The sight caused Rebekkah to laugh and ask, "Um, what are you doing Godfrey?"

Unable to focus on anything other than his internal conflict, Godfrey became less animated and looked downward.

Rebekkah's eyebrows squished together and she said, "Are you alright?"

With his head still down, Godfrey shrugged his shoulders and blurted out, "Can I ask you a question?"

"Sure. Shoot." Rebekkah said.

"You knew how much I hated Carson so why was it so easy for you to go through with the plan? I mean, you really went through with it. You married him and had to pretend to be in love with him...you slept with him. I'm just wondering how you were able to do it?"

Rebekkah made a quick glance at Godfrey, turned away, and then turn to him again saying, "It was the hardest thing I had to do but I did it because I knew just how much you hated him. What better way to get revenge on someone than with someone they trust? I did it for you Godfrey, I did it for us. Do you know how hard it was for me to pretend to like him, to love him? On the outside, he has a lot going for him but, he's quite empty on the inside. Not only that, all he talked about was his ex-wife. Imagine how I felt living in her shadow...can you? Why do you think I left the first time, it just got to be too much."

Grabbing a pillow, Rebekkah held it close and clutched it tightly, "But here's the thing, you want to how I was able to do it so easily but do you realize you pimped me out to him? I could ask you, how were you able to so easily let me go through with it? I have battle scars for what I went through, he shot me once and tried to do it again. You see Godfrey, there's always a different way to look at things."

A slight chill came over Godfrey but it wasn't because of the ocean air, his emotions heightened and he began to feel on edge. A deep, pained breath escaped his mouth as he closed his eyes and began to weep.

"Rebekkah, baby...I'm so sorry. I never thought about it that way. I was so caught up in how I felt about Carson that I never considered anything beyond my own hatred. This is awful. I don't know if you can ever forgive me but I beg of you to do so." Godfrey cried.

Godfrey desired to come clean, he wanted to confess, he wished he could go back and change everything but he couldn't bring himself to do it. He figured he'd spend the rest of his life trying to right his wrongs with Rebekkah and the baby. He'd devote his life to making up for his indiscretions.

Placing her hands on his face, Rebekkah said, "I more than forgive you Godfrey...I love you. Through thick and thin, you've always been there for me. You've loved me when no one else would and when I couldn't even love myself. You love me in spite of everything I've done in my life. Which is why - ."

Godfrey interrupted Rebekkah by saying, "Wait a minute, you make it sound like you've done such horrible things. We all make mistakes and you shouldn't feel like you've done such bad things that would make me stop loving you. There is nothing you could do to make me not love you."

"Thanks Godfrey and if you'd let me finish, I've made a decision about something and I want to tell you. I've been thinking and I think it's better for all parties considered for me to drop this whole paternity thing with Carson. I don't even care if you do the test anymore because in the grand scheme of things, it doesn't matter. When I was growing up, I used to hear my mother say, sometimes it doesn't matter who you love but who loves you and I know without a shadow of a doubt you love me. It's simple, you and I love each other and together we are going to love and raise this baby. So let's not even worry about anything else, what do you think about that?" Rebekkah said.

Godfrey pounced onto Rebekkah, hugging and kissing her, repeatedly saying, "I love you baby." With tears streaming down his face, his shiny cheeks burned from smiling. "You have no idea how this news makes me feel; you have made me the happiest man alive." He screamed.

Embracing one another Rebekkah said, "Had I known that, I would have told you a long time ago."

"Oh my goodness, we have to celebrate. Do you feel like going out later? I know we were going to hang outside for a while today but you think you'll want to go and do a little partying later?" Godfrey asked.

Rebekkah's starry eyes looked deeply into Godfrey's and said, "As long as I'm with my man, I'm down for anything. I'll party all night as long as I'm with you."

Chapter 50

"I'm so glad you were able to come with me...you know to help me drive and all."

Bishop Montgomery smiled and said, "You're still sticking with that line huh?" Kissing Delores' hand, he looked over and said, "I'd drive across a desert if I had to if it meant spending time with you."

Enjoying the warmth of Bishop's tender touch, Delores extended the hand play by squeezing his.

Each day since the movie screening, the two had been together, making the most of their time. Their flirtation had brought them to Delores' home where she needed to check on things.

The short stay was filled to the brim, Delores managed to handle her business, show Bishop around, and even introduced him to her children...as an old friend of course.

"Can I ask you something?" Delores asked.

"Anything. What's on your mind?" Bishop replied.

Taking a slight pause before answering, Delores said, "Well, I guess being back home brought up so old memories, seeing my children and my grandchildren made me think of Charles. I really miss him. I was wondering how have you been dealing with losing your wife, how do you deal with the grief?"

Bishop Montgomery exhaled loudly, "I guess you can say, I haven't been dealing with it very well. It's been hard but apparently the good Lord sees fit to wake me up each day and each day I keep trying to find the meaning of what's next in my life. It's like, I buried my wife but I haven't buried my feelings or my marriage. I miss Regina like none other, the problem is, she's not coming back and I think I've finally come to that realization."

On the drive back, an oldie but goodie came on the radio, it was from the group they went to see in concert, *The Harmonics.* The group was known for their ability to harmonize like no other group around. Hearing the song was a welcomed distraction from the pair trading their grief-stricken stories. Turning up the volume, Delores pulled a brush from her bag and eased up next to Bishop so they could sing, harmonize together in her make shift microphone. There were so many ooh ooh oohs and la la las sung between the two of them, the couple could not stop laughing.

Bishop and Delores let loose, they allowed themselves to be silly and goofy and they sang their hearts out.

Bishop's sidesplitting laughter caused him to say, "I think after that, we need to stop and get a bite to eat. I have sung myself hungry, what do you think?"

Wiping the happy tears from eyes, still tickled from the song, Delores said, "I agree."

Walking inside the restaurant, Bishop thought nothing of it and grabbed Delores' hand, they walked inside hand in hand.

Instead of sitting across from him, Delores decided to sit next to Bishop Montgomery.

"Thank you again for coming, it really means a lot." Delores said.

"No, thank you for inviting me. I can't think of the last time I had this much fun, I almost don't want this trip to end." Bishop replied.

Delores opened her mouth and then closed it, she pulled at her ear and then decided to ask some questions to gain more insight into Bishop's comment.

"Can I ask you something? What are we doing here?" Delores asked.

Oblivious to Delores' true intent, Bishop said, "Getting ready to eat, did you want to go somewhere else?"

"No silly." Delores said chuckling. "I mean, you and I, what are we doing? I guess I feel too old to say the word, dating. Besides you, my husband was the only other man, I've ever dated."

Now clued in, Bishop apologized, "I'm sorry, I guess I didn't pick up what you were saying." Shifting in the booth, Bishop turned to Delores and said, "I don't know how to date. After you, Regina and I were practically arranged so I'm not the expert here at all." Bishop took Delores' hand and said, "I only know how to be married."

Making a hmmm noise in her throat, Delores felt a flutter in her belly and it wasn't from the hunger pains.

With her lips close to his ears, Delores whispered, "Did you mean what you said about not wanting this trip to end?"

Bishop returned a whispered response saying, "Yes, I did."

The closeness they shared brought them to the brink of kissing, they still hadn't indulged and explored that part of their relationship. The moment was barely distracted when the server brought their food to the table. Aware of the vibes at the table, the server delivered the food and left, leaving Delores and Bishop to continue.

Feeling impulsive, Delores said, "If you don't want it to end, what are you going to do about it?"

Playfully, Bishop said, "What do you want me to do about it?"

The inviting, yet back and forth banter between them was enchanting.

Seeing an opportunity, Delores asked, "Do you believe in spontaneity, living in the moment?" Pulling back somewhat, Delores said, "I want you to look out the window and if you see the same thing I do, I say we go for it."

Ready to embrace the unknown, Bishop searched for what Delores was referring to. He studied the landscape as if he was preparing for a final exam and then he stopped with a smile. He'd found it.

Rushing her words, Delores said, "So, what do you think?"

Turning his head towards Delores, he said, "I think we should do. Let's go for it."

Without eating their food, Bishop threw a large sum of cash on the table and he and Delores ran out of the restaurant laughing. They were enthusiastic for what was to come. Lacking thought or reason, in an instant they'd decided to take a chance down a road they were excited to see where it might lead.

Across the street, Bishop and Delores stood outside a tiny building, "Our Little Wedding Chapel."

Lock, stock, and barrel, the two walked inside.

Chapter 51

"Hey Grandma, there's a package here for and they said you need to sign for it."

"Okay baby, I'll be right there." Mother Montgomery said.

Cayden-James stood outside of his grandmother's room and waited for her to come out. He walked with her to the front door.

"Hello ma'am, I have a package here for you and it requires your signature for delivery."

"I didn't order anything; do you know who it's from?"

"No ma'am, there is no return address or name on it."

"Alright young man; I'll sign for it."

Mother Montgomery retrieved her package and Cayden-James closed the door. He asked, "So grandma, are you excited about the luncheon tomorrow?"

"I am baby, I am. I think it's going to be real nice, I hope we can make Regina proud. I hate she's not here, I miss her so much." Mother Montgomery replied.

"I know; I miss her too. I think about her every day but I know she'd be proud of you and she's here with us in spirit." Cayden-James comforted.

"Well, grandma is going to go back and lie down, I want to make sure I'm well rested for tomorrow." Mother Montgomery added.

On the way to her room, she passed Cherie in the hallway who was texting on her phone and bumped into her.

"Excuse you. I see nasty Cherie has turned into zombie Cherie, you might want to take your eyes off that phone and watch where you are going." Mother scolded.

Humbled, Cherie spoke in a quiet voice, "I'm sorry, I really didn't mean to bump into you. I'm stressing because I've been going back and forth with Monica today." Cherie explained.

Tucking the package under her arm, Mother Montgomery asked, "What's going on with Monica?"

"According to her, she says the label says it's time for me to go back on the road, like starting next week and I'm not so sure I'm ready to go."

Thinking back to her previous conversation with Monica, Mother Montgomery inquired, "Well, how long before you think you'll be ready?"

Breathing a heavy sigh and falling up against the wall, Cherie said, "I don't know grandma. Since I've been here, I've been thinking a lot about my life. I realize there is a price to pay for road life and someone I know paid dearly...with their life."

Mother Montgomery stepped towards Cherie and hugged her. From elder to junior, Mother's loving arms caused a dam to break within Cherie, she began to cry. Cherie was responding internally rather than from external persona.

Rubbing her hand through her hair, Mother said, "It's alright, you let it all out. Everything is going to be okay. Grandma will make sure of that. Now, let me ask you this, do you still feel up to singing at the luncheon tomorrow?"

"Yes ma'am, I feel like it's the least I can do. Hopefully, I can do something that'll make my auntiemama Regina smile down from heaven."

Wiping Cherie's tears, Mother said, "Well, like I told Cayden-James, grandma needs to and get some rest. You might need to get some too. Tomorrow is going to be a big day for us."

Walking into her room, Mother Montgomery tossed the package onto her desk. She laid down and tried to fall asleep. She found herself tossing and turning, unable to find the necessary rest she desired. Each time she tossed, her eyes fell on the package. With every turn, she noticed the package.

Feeling as if the package was calling out to her and since she wasn't able to sleep anyway, Mother Montgomery got up and opened the envelope.

Emptying the contents, Mother saw a note, it read:

"You don't know me but your grandson, Carson wanted me to mail this to you. There's no need to trace it because it has gone through several people to get to me and now to you. In the video you will watch there is no metadata on the file so you can't trace that either. Bottom line, Carson doesn't want anyone trying to locate him. He does want you to know he loves you and trusts you'll know what to do. As you watch, you'll soon realize everything you need to know will be discovered in the video file."

Along with the note was a jump drive that Mother Montgomery plugged into her computer.

Watching the video, Mother Montgomery's mouth fell to the ground and her hands flew to her chest.

Closing out the file, Mother Montgomery carefully repackaged the contents of the envelope.

Grabbing her phone, she placed a call to Monica, inviting her to the luncheon.

Chapter 52

"How are you feeling being here as the new kid on the block to my dead wife's luncheon?"

Delores lowered her head and said, "I'm fine, well, I guess I'll be fine."

Standing close enough to share a kiss, Bishop whispered, "Well, you look beautiful. I'm praying and hoping you feel comfortable, as you know, this will now become your life."

Taking in a deep breath, Delores said, "I know but eventually. I'm glad we thought better of ourselves, came to our senses, and decided to take things slow...give this dating thing a try."

At the chapel, in the middle of picking out a wedding package, both Delores and Bishop decided this wasn't what they wanted...not like that. They decided they would give themselves some time to get to know one another again and let things unfold naturally. They were both happy with the decision and walked back over to the restaurant and this time, ordered their food to go.

Delores arrived ahead of time to help with any last minute details, she wanted to make sure Mother Montgomery knew, she was there to help. Delores joined, Ali and Lillian in the kitchen. Each woman in their own right looked amazing, from their stunning attire to the perfectly coiffed hair to their fabulous make-up, each of the ladies were determined to represent well at the luncheon.

Preparations were well underway outside, just the way, Regina had done in the past. The hustle and bustle was in full effect on the grounds of the Montgomery estate.

Normally, in previous years, Regina would welcome women from all over the country to her home for this occasion and by this particular time, she would see some arrive a little early to fellowship with her prior to event. This year, no one arrived early.

Getting nervous, Mother Montgomery huffed, "I can't believe people aren't showing up. We are about to start in a few minutes."

Delores walked over to Mother Montgomery and said, "Don't get too upset. You've done a wonderful job preserving the legacy of Lady Regina and I'm sure who's supposed to be here will be here."

Lillian stepped in and echoed Delores' sentiment, "I agree Mother, everything looks beautiful, you've done an outstanding job. I say we make a pact that no matter who shows up, we are still going to have a great time today."

The ladies were all escorted out to the enormous white tent where a few women were signing in. Inside the tent, Mother Montgomery received a call. The speaker for the luncheon was calling to cancel.

Mother Montgomery handled the excuse with grace and offered her prayers towards the situation. She stood shaking her head.

Paying attention, Delores walked over and asked, "Is everything okay, are you alright?"

"I'm alright if having your speaker cancel on you at the very last minute is okay, then I'm alright. Supposedly her daughter is sick and she can't make it, so now we're left without a speaker." Mother Montgomery shouted.

Lillian walked over and asked, "What seems to be the problem?"

Delores explained to Lillian the situation as a few more women trickled in for registration.

Mother Montgomery inhaled and then exhaled, she looked around and said, "All is well, one monkey won't stop this show. These women aren't showing up like I thought and it's okay. I see they must have only been coming because of Regina not for real impartation. Nevertheless, we will continue on in the name of the Lord."

Ali spoke up and said, "Well, what are you going to do about a speaker, who will you get to speak at such short notice?"

Mother Montgomery looked squarely at Ali and simply said, "Me. I'm going to speak. As I said, one monkey don't stop, won't stop, this show. And whoever ain't here, well...let's just get started."

As a few more women entered the tent, Mother Montgomery gave the signal to start the luncheon. With the less than expected crowd and the cancelled speaker, Mother Montgomery decided to do things differently. She gave the order to have the food served immediately. She wanted a few minutes to step aside and pray. On her way outside, she spotted Monica who walked in with Cherie.

While everyone gathered enjoyed their lunch, Mother Montgomery was praying. When she wasn't praying, she was coordinating and orchestrating things.

Lillian walked up to the microphone, she stepped in to say she would introduce Mother Montgomery as the speaker.

Mother walked back in right as Lillian began speaking. "Ladies, since we are changing things up a bit, we will serve dessert after Mother Montgomery blesses us. Is that alright with everyone?"

All of the ladies responded in unison, "Yes."

As a seasoned saint, Mother Montgomery graced the platform with class and sophistication. She'd prayed and she was now open to whatever the Lord wanted her to say.

Grabbing the mic, she instructed everyone to move in closer to her, "We're going to do things a little differently this time. We have a small number here and so we all are going to be one big happy family and gather around. We have a nice intimate setting and I'm going to talk to you all from right here." Mother motioned for someone to bring her a chair so she could sit among the women who'd formed a half circle.

Smiling, Mother Montgomery said, "The devil thinks he has a place in my life, I keep trying to tell him he doesn't. But every now and then, I have to show him better than I can tell him. Does anyone know what I'm talking about?"

Some of the ladies smiled, while others clapped and agreed with Mother. Some women were flat out amused she was going to be speaking.

"So today, we are all here because my beloved daughter-in-law, Regina...may God bless the dead, started this luncheon years ago and I wanted to keep it going in her honor. Now, everyone didn't show up like I thought they would but that's okay. The bible says, where two or three are gathered together in His name, there He is in the midst. As I look around, we have more than two or three so I think we're going to be just fine." Mother Montgomery said, laying her foundation.

Mother took her seat in the center of the semi-circle, she said, "I just want to talk with you all for a moment if I may. It's been a while since the last time I've had an opportunity to share in a forum like this but I believe the Lord has something He wants me to impart. Are you ladies ready to receive? If so, let me hear you shout, amen."

Those assembled all shouted in agreement, "Amen."

"Alright, well, let me ask you all something. How many of you sometimes focus your attention more on your problems than on the goodness of Jesus?" Surveying the room, Mother Montgomery said, "Okay, looks like at some point or another, we all have done that, we are all guilty of doing that. Here's the thing though, when we do that, what we are saying with our lives is that, God, we don't trust what You are doing and we're not sure if You love us enough or if You really are in control of our lives. If truth be told, that is what we are doing. You all may as well tell the truth and shame the devil because, that is what we do when we focus on the problems rather than the problem solver. I can say this because I've lived it. However, over the years, Mother has decided to trust God no matter what. Very rarely do I get upset over trials that come up in my life. The bible warns us not to be surprised when trials come to test us, in fact, it says, fiery trials. Lord have mercy, sometimes these trials can get too hot to handle."

Everyone laughed at Mother Montgomery's witty and entertaining style of delivery.

She took a sip of water and continued, "In my lifetime, I've been through some fiery trials but with the help of the Lord, I made it through. Right now, my family is faced with a fiery trial but I have a peace about how this situation will work out because I trust God." Mother Montgomery looked over at

Monica and Cherie and said, "I believe Him and His word when it says, all things are working together for my good. I recognize that down through the years, the Lord has been good to me and if you look back, you'll see the same. I can pinpoint in each trial and tribulation that He was there, even when I didn't feel Him, He was there. Psalms 139:8 shows us there is no place we can go where He isn't there...no place."

Mother Montgomery decided she wanted to stand and walk around a bit, she wanted to get up close and personal with each woman. "When I consider all I've seen and gone through, I'm reminded of when King David said, "I once was old but I've never seen the righteous forsaken, nor his seed begging for bread. It's a familiar passage but it the truth of my life. I know I look good but Mother is old, on some days I feel real old. However, that doesn't take away the fact I know God is with me always. He was good to me when I was young and He's good to me now that I'm old. His hand has always been upon my life, even when I didn't deserve it. He's blessed me when I've belittled others."

Mother Montgomery walked over to Delores and grabbed her hand. Looking at Delores she said, "Oh but I thank God for His grace and mercy to get things right, to apologize, and set the record straight.

A swell in Delores' heart caused a small tear to pool in the corner of her eyes.

"Ladies, if you hear nothing from me today, I want you to know God loves you so much, His love is everlasting and it never fails. I'm here my dear sisters to declare His wondrous works and the power of His love. When family leaves you, when that husband says he leaving, when you feel all alone and feel like no one understands, trust me when I tell you, He does. Even in my old age, according to Psalms 71:9, I have an assurance He will not forsake me when my strength is failing. He will be with me until the very end and even when I close my eyes for the last time, I'll open them up in the arms of Jesus. So as you can see I'm planted, I've taken root in the house of the LORD and I'm going to continue to flourish in His courts. Even in my old age, I'm still yielding fruit, I'm healthy and I'm fresh[9]. Oh y'all didn't know, you better ask somebody about Mother Betty Montgomery. I'm here to declare He's my rock and in Him there is no unrighteousness."

Mother Montgomery found her stride, she was nearing the end of her time of sharing.

"There is no unrighteousness in Him and I love this so because back to what David said, I once was young but now I'm old and I've never seen the righteous forsaken nor his seed beg for bread. It is impossible for the Lord to forsake me, He just won't do it and I know that no matter what I may come up against or what my seed comes up against, He's right there because He delights in justice and the righteous are never forsaken. For each of you here, I admonish you to get this type of settling in your spirit, that no matter what's going on...Trust God. I leave you my dear sisters with this, in life, you are going to go through some things but be strong, courageous, and firm; don't be afraid because it is the Lord, our God who goes

---

[9] **Psalms 92:13-14**: *"Planted in the house of the LORD, they will flourish in the courts of our God. They will still yield fruit in old age; They shall be full of sap and very green. To declare that the LORD is upright; He is my rock, and there is no unrighteousness in Him."* (**NIV**)

with you. Always remember, He'll never fail or forsake you[10].
God loves you and so do I. Be encouraged."

The women all stood up and gave Mother Montgomery a standing ovation, they all were able to see scripture personified in the wisdom she shared. Right before taking her seat, she said, "We're going to have that dessert now and while you all are enjoying it, I want for my granddaughter, National Recording Artist, Cherie Monet to come and bless us with a song.

---

[10] **Deuteronomy 31:6:** *"Be strong and courageous. Do not be afraid or terrified because of them, for the LORD your God goes with you; he will never leave you nor forsake you."* (**NIV**)

Chapter 53

The servers took to the floor and doled out the dessert, a decadent display of brownie a la mode, featuring Ali's infamous brownies. Mother Montgomery ordered up a batch from Ali to have served at the luncheon.

As everyone delighted in the final course of the luncheon, Cherie prepared herself to sing. Monica pulled out her phone to video the performance, she thought it would be a great piece to place on social media for Cherie's fans in anticipation for her upcoming tour.

Towards the end of finishing her brownie, Lillian stood up to introduce Cherie.

Cherie approached the platform in a long, spaghetti strapped, maxi dress that sparkled when she moved. She was a bit fidgety but she blew air out of her mouth to calm the butterflies in her stomach. She opened her mouth and said, "I just want to thank my grandmother for putting this luncheon on. Despite everything that's happened, she did an amazing job and when I tell you all she means every word she spoke, she does. This woman don't play and she speaks the truth...even when you don't want to hear it."

Mother Montgomery held up a fist in Cherie's direction and they both smiled.

"I've been here in Vino for a while and I've had an opportunity to spend a lot of time with her lately and grandma Montgomery, I want you to know I love you and even when you think I'm not listening...I am. I'm here to sing this song for you all today but I want to dedicate this song to my grandmother. It's something I've been working on called, *He Still Chose Me.*"

Placing the microphone in the stand, Cherie belted out a few notes and everyone dropped their forks to listen to her. Her voice demanded attention, her lyrics required consideration. It had been a while since Cherie had used her gift but she opened up and allowed the Lord to flow through her in song. The musicians followed her flawlessly and she sang with an anointing that caused some women to weep. The hairs on Mother Montgomery's arm stood up, she was witnessing transformation taking place within Cherie. She could tell Cherie's heart was changing, it was tender and open to the Lord. Cherie was tapping into the redemptive work through the forgiveness of sins through the blood of Christ Jesus.

Just as Mother Montgomery was noticing Cherie's conversion, so was Monica but she felt differently than Mother Montgomery. While Mother was rejoicing for what she was seeing, Monica was becoming uncomfortable at the same sight.

Cherie sang a few bars of the following:

...Got a taste of real life
Trying to be free
Not realizing, God's timing is key
Now, I know, it's not cliché
God will keep you even when you stray
I've been down, even ashamed
Turned my back on Him, yet He protected me
In my sin; He still chose me
With His blood; He wiped all my guilt away

Now, I know, how much He loves me
How He keeps me in every single way
In my sin; He still chose me
Now, I know, how his blood has cleansed me
In my sin; He still chose me...

With her hands in the air, Cherie reached down deep and sung her heart out in a perfect pitch and towards a soulful crescendo.

The original song was powerful and moving, there was not a dry eye in the tent and everyone was on their feet.

Chapter 54

"Oh Mother Montgomery, the luncheon turned out beautifully, I'm so glad, I could be here to take part in it."

"Lillian, dear, I appreciate all of your help, you've been such a blessing." Mother Montgomery said.

After the luncheon, a few of the women hung back to fellowship back up at the house, including Monica.

"Um, Cherie...do you mind if I speak with you alone?" Monica asked.

As tired as Mother Montgomery was, she knew her work wasn't done, she still had things to do. Keeping a careful eye on Monica and Cherie, she watched where they walked to.

"What is it Monica? I thought I was clear, I'm not ready to go back out on the road. In fact, I'm not sure if I'll ever be ready?" Cherie confessed.

Rubbing the back of her neck, Monica groaned, "Cherie, we've talked about this and you can't just up and decide you don't want to perform anymore. You signed a contract with us and in case you didn't know it, we essentially own you. The label has been trying to be patient and give you some time over this whole Blue situation but you've got to get it together...and quick."

"Does his death mean nothing to you, I mean, is that all you and the label care about it is performing? I mean, a man died here and you are here talking to me about going back on the road. I don't get it."

Monica's harsh squint matched her comment, "Well if you ask me, Blue got what he deserved." The words were out of her mouth before she could take them back.

"Why would you say that?" Cherie exclaimed.

Before Monica could answer, a voice called out, "Honey dip."

Without realizing it, Monica turned around and answered, "Yes?"

Mother Montgomery walked up, speaking slowly to emphasize her point saying, "Yeah honey dip, we all want to know why you would say little boy blue got what he deserved."

Standing directly behind Mother Montgomery stood two detectives, the ones who'd questioned Cherie, Bishop Montgomery, Cayden-James.

Glancing around looking for answers, both Cherie and Monica said, "What's going on here?"

Mother Montgomery instructed everyone to follow her. Walking up next to a trembling Monica, she grabbed her hand and said, "I want you to walk with me."

Inside the study, Mother Montgomery had everything she needed setup.

Warning the group, Mother Montgomery said, "I need to let you know, what you are about to hear and see may contain some graphic content.

Unsure of what to expect, Monica asked if she could be excused to use the restroom. Mother Montgomery looked at her and said, "This won't take long dear, just give Mother a few minutes and I'll be out of everyone's way."

Monica's intuition kicked in, she had feelings something wasn't quite right. Her muscles began to tense up and her heartbeat started to race.

Mother clicked the mouse at the computer and all of a sudden everyone heard from none other than Carson. Turning up the speakers, Mother Montgomery made it so that Carson's voice filled the room. His face wasn't visible, only his voice and he said, "My name is Carson Eugene Montgomery IV and what I have to say is very important."

By this time, Monica knew she was in trouble. She tried to make a run for it but Mother Montgomery had taken all kinds of precautions, two armed men were standing outside of the study and apprehended her.

"I went to pay a visit to Johnson Blue, Cherie's drummer. She'd told me he was harassing her about something and I told her I'd go and check him out. Before I left to meet up with him, I tried calling Cherie's managers. Cherie had mentioned she was waiting to hear back from them concerning this guy so I wanted to see if they knew anything. The only person I was able to track down was Monica. She wasn't aware of the situation between Cherie and Blue until I'd mentioned it." Carson explained.

Handcuffed in a corner, Monica yelled out, "He's lying. Don't believe a word he says, they're all lies."

Looking back over her shoulder, Mother Montgomery said, "Don't worry honey dip, you'll have your day in court to tell your side of the story."

The video continued with Carson speaking, "The next day, I flew to see the guy, I just went to see why he was bothering Cherie the way he was and to see if there was anything I could do. When I got there, no one answered the door. I walked around and was able to convince the apartment manager that I was a family member and was concerned about him and needed access to his apartment. I must've put on the charm because it worked, she let me in."

Cayden-James and Bishop both looked at each other and shook their heads at Carson's comment.

Continuing on he said, "I snooped around his apartment but didn't really find anything, then all of a sudden, I heard two people arguing down the hallway and I ran into his front closet. I stood in the closet and waited to see what was going on and I heard Monica yelling at Blue, cursing him out and saying things like she couldn't believe he cheated on her by making those videos. Based on their argument, apparently Monica and Blue were in a relationship and she didn't know anything about the videos until I told her. I was in the closet listening to her confront him about them."

Cherie's neck bent forward, her eyes widened as she said, "What a minute. Can you pause that for a second?" Mother Montgomery obliged. Turning towards Monica, Cherie asked, "Am I understanding this correctly that you and Blue were in a relationship?"

With her hands behind her back, Monica raised up out of her seat and tried to lunge towards Cherie and said, "Yes and you were sleeping with him, you stanking whore." The two men slammed Monica back down to her seat. Cherie backed off in a state dismay, feeling let down.

Mother Montgomery started Carson's audio again, "The crazy part about all of this is, through the vented closet, I recorded the entire ordeal. From the argument, to Monica hitting him over the head and knocking him to the ground to her pouring honey all over his body. Here's the real messed up part, this chick brought in with her real African killer bees. She pulled a box from her bag and released them inside the apartment. She tortured that poor man, she demanded he tell her where the video was. She grabbed his phone and left."

Carson had configured the video to where he'd merged the video he'd taken at the apartment and combined it with his account of the events. The next part of the video showed Blue covered in bees trying to swat them off and with no luck, he ran out of his apartment screaming. So yes, I was there but no I didn't kill him. I never even got a chance to talk to him. As you can see on the video, Monica is the one who murdered Johnson Blue."

Mother Montgomery stopped the video and turned around to Cherie who was sobbing. Bishop Montgomery, Cayden-James, and Mother all leaned in and hugged her.

Bishop threw his head back and said, "Praise the Lord I'm glad that's over. Now, all I need to know is where my son is, why he left, and when is he coming home?" Smiling at his mother he said, "Detective Montgomery do you know the answers to those questions?"

Mother answered by saying, "If you watch the rest of the video he says he loves us but he doesn't know if or when he'll be back in Vino. He said a lot has happened and he needs some time to himself, I think seeing such a tragic death has shaken him up. I can't even imagine what he must be going through."

Cayden-James spoke up and said, "Well, at least we know he's alive and he sounds like he's doing okay. His voice sounded strong so prayerfully he's managing his illness. But grandma, I just have to say, you are one bad mamma jamma. If I ever go missing, I want you on my case, do you hear me? You cracked this case wide open."

Mother Montgomery looked at her family and said, "Monica kind of told on herself, she was popping up too much. She was hurt by that young man but she had to protect her business too. But son, all I can tell you is that when I pray, the Lord listens. I called on Him in my time of need and He answered my call. He never leaves me nor forsakes me, He always remembers this here 'ole Mother. He favors me and with Him, I'm UNFORSAKEN."

Epilogue

"So, a lot has happened, huh? Did you all think I murdered Blue? I hope not, I hope by now you all know I'm too self-centered for that. I've done some bad things in my life but I'm pretty sure murdering someone is where I draw the line."

"I'm sure you have a few questions and I'll try my best to answer them. Do you want to know why I filed the petition against Scarlett? It's like this, I filed because after Rebekkah betrayed me, I was so angry and I let my feelings get the best of me. Knowing I have a son out there with my DNA began to eat away at me. I couldn't eat, I couldn't sleep, I couldn't do anything but think about him. The small picture I saw on the cellphone was singed into my brain. His little face that looked like mine flashed across my mind every day and so yes, I went back on my word and fired off a petition. I knew I didn't have a shot but I was hurt. It really is true when they say, hurt people, hurt people. Truth of the matter is, I don't know why I keep hurting Scarlett, I guess it's also true when they say you hurt the ones you love the most."

"In a way, I've given up on trying to get custody of him because let's be real, I'm in no position to take care of him and I can barely take care of myself. Which is why, I've traveled far away to an alternative treatment facility, one that specializes in my type of Leukemia. That probably answers one of your other questions."

"I have to say, seeing that young man die like that shook me up, I grew up privileged, I didn't grow up seeing things like that. So really and truly, after seeing that, I remembered that book I'd given to Scarlett and I did what I made her do, I disappeared. I have to say, I'm enjoying going places and people not knowing who I am or where I've come from. I'm seeing life through a whole new perspective. Where do you think I am? If you think you know, send an email to shakirabelieves@gmail.com and see if you're correct. I will say this though, even though some of you might think this is the end, I'm here to tell you, I'm not saying good-bye, I'm only saying, see you later."

Psalms 37:25

"I was young and now I am old, yet I have never seen the righteous forsaken or their children begging bread. (NIV)"

About the Author

Shakira R. Thompson, a natural born storyteller who submitted to her God-given talents and in doing so, God showed up and made her a BELIEVER. He's transformed her into an author, publisher, and entrepreneur.

She is the founder of Believer's Choice Media, an inspirational content company dedicated to encouraging believers to live the life they were created to live on earth and beyond. She's penned five, well-received inspirational fiction novels with a sixth on the way.

With a renewed sense of purpose, Shakira is not only writing and speaking, she's living...living her life according to Ephesians 2:10:

"For we are his workmanship, created in Christ Jesus unto good works, which God hath before ordained that we should walk in them." (KJV)

Shakira is a proud Alumni of Florida A&M University in Tallahassee, Florida where she holds a B.S in Business Administration as well as an M.B.A. with a concentration in Supply Chain Management.

Shakira has always delved in the world of real estate, but most recently made it official. She is a Realtor®, licensed in the State of Florida, where she's the listing agent for EquityPro. Naturally, she' s expanding the Believer's Choice brand and is in the process of developing Believer's Choice Realty, LLC.

Living her life with purpose has pushed her into her latest venture, co-hosting *The Dee Lee Show,* where she has the opportunity to encourage BELIEVERS over the airwaves.

Although Shakira may wear many hats these days, the most important role to her, is that of wife and mother.

Born and raised in Fernandina Beach, Florida, she now resides in Orlando, Florida with her family.

A Sneak Peek
The Missing Ingredient

"So you leave out tomorrow, huh?"

"Yeah man and I can't wait. I feel like I've been preparing for this my whole life. I plan to be the last man standing when it's all over. You just wait and see."

Bailee "Bay-leaf" Jones, an upcoming coming chef gave himself the nickname, "Bay Leaf" and he was one day away from taping a new reality show entitled, "Sliced." The show would feature chefs from all around the country who would compete for a prize package to include promotion, publicity, and major prosperity. Winning the competition would catapult the winner into a rock star, celebrity chef.

Seated at the bar of a very noisy and crowded Casey's Lounge, Bailee tried speaking over the crowd, he continuously shouted out his predictions to his brother, Andrew. The two brothers toasted to Bailee's strategy of *slicing* his competition at the knees and sending them home, one by one.

"And you'll be gone for how long again?" Andrew asked.

Chugging another drink, with slurred speech, Bailee said, "I'll be gone for about three weeks. The show will tape for about two weeks but I plan to take full advantage of my time in the big apple, N.Y.C. here I come baby. If I make it to the finals, I'll be there for the third week."

Andrew shook his head and said, "I think you've had enough brother. It's time for you to take it in."

Bailee protested, "No bro, I'm good. Aren't you having a good time with me tonight? I'm going to be on my "A" game while I'm out there filming. I'm not going to be drinking the entire time I'm there so I want to live it up a little tonight."

"Exactly." Andrew agreed. "Which is why you need to be sharp tomorrow, not recovering from a hangover. You want to make a good impression don't you?"

Normally, Bailee was quite confident, in fact, his friends and family would likely describe him as having an overly confident view of himself, however, the weight of the competition, the fear of the unknown was causing him severe anxiety. Having drinks and hanging out with his older brother, who played dual roles in his life as best friend, confidant, and biggest supporter was the only way he knew to relieve his rising stress levels.

Barely able to open his eyes, Bailee answered slowly, "Yes. I'm going to make a great impression. The producers said I nailed my audition which is why they picked me to be on the show. I am going to crush my competition; this show was made for me to win it. I promise I'm going to win...I have to win. Man, this competition means everything to me. I've been training in my kitchen for weeks, I've been dreaming of new recipes and trying them out every day man. If I win, no when I win, this could literally change my life so guess what, failure is not an option. I have to win Andrew, I have to."

Laughing at his drunk brother babbling Andrew coddled his brother and said, "Yes, I know Bailee, you're going to win."

Trying to offer Bailee some advice, Andrew said, "Hey listen, you're pretty smashed right now so I don't know if you'll remember any of this but I want to tell you something." Getting up close in Bailee's face, Andrew said, "Yes, you are a gifted chef, you got the goods man but you know it and that my friend can be your down fall. You too cocky man, you are your own man and I can't tell you what to do but don't go in there trying to be a show boat. Just do what you do and everything else will fall into place."

Inebriation wasn't enough to make Bailee step back and take heed to the wise words of his brother, he laughed them off, dismissed him and said, "Yes and that kind of talk is why you're still where you at...but I love you though."

Grabbing Andrew by the head, he held in a head-lock saying, "Yeah, yeah, and I love you to, you jerk. Good luck man."

••••

"Are you all packed up and ready to go?"

"I sure am, I probably won't be able to sleep tonight because I'm so excited."

Carly Anderson, the light of her parent's life, a young chef with big dreams and a passion for food was already making waves in the press.

The local newspaper in her hometown was present to do a feature story on her and about her being selected to be on the show, "Sliced."

Growing up in a family of restauranteurs, Carly developed a love for food at an early age in her parent's Southern cuisine restaurant. She had an opportunity to wake up to tantalizing smells born from Southern comforts, she paid attention to the details of baking perfect pound cakes and pies, and she gravitated to the sounds of popping grease. Carly relished in the magic created in a down-home kitchen. Her culinary pedigree was fueled with love of home and family and everyone believed Carly would showcase that on the show.

"That was a really nice interview you did Carly; we are so proud of you." Elizabeth Andrews said.

Smiling, Carly said, "Thanks mom, I pray everything works out well while I'm gone."

Elizabeth looked at her daughter and said, "Everything will work out how it's supposed to. You see my dear, you have an unfair advantage."

"What do you mean mom?" Carly asked.

Reaching for her bible, Elizabeth said, "Oh Carly, you know, it's simple. For our God has already blessed you according to His divine power, He's given everything pertaining to life and godliness[11]. You have this thing in the bag honey. Not to mention, we also believe in the promises of God that says your gift will make room for you and bring you before great men[12]. And last but not least, you have a praying family who will be praying for you all the way. Listen to me, you can do this, you can handle this. I want you to go there and let your light shine so that men might see your good works and glorify our Father in heaven[13]. Do you hear me? You will be just fine; you were born for this. By virtue of your name, you are our little champion. We named you that because you are a fighter, a winner. You know the story; I've told you many times how you made it through a traumatic birth. So if you can make it through that, trust me honey, you can make it through anything."

---

[11] **2 Peter 1:3:** *"According as his divine power hath given unto us all things that pertain unto life and godliness, through the knowledge of him that hath called us to glory and virtue:"* (**KJV**)

[12] **Proverbs 18:16**: *"A man's gift maketh room for him, and bringeth him before great men."* (**KJV**)

[13] **Matthew 5:16**: *"Let your light so shine before men, that they may see your good works, and glorify your Father which is in heaven.* (**KJV**)

Elizabeth's exhortation was the calming force Carly needed as she set out to be the winner of the show, "Sliced."

~ *The Missing Ingredient*

Note from the Author

Final Thoughts

This is the last book in the Psalms 37 Novel series but I can assure you, it will not the last time we hear from the Watsons, the Montgomerys, or the Hartgroves. I'm not sure where we will go next but you can be certain, they will be returning.

Writing this series has been an amazing journey for me, a major milestone, and a dream come true. For years, due to my own insecurities, I sat on a God-given gift because I was too scared. I was too afraid to put myself out there for people to judge the merits of my work.

You will never know how happy I am, I decided to take a leap of faith and write. Since, I decided to overcome those fears, I've now written five books with three more in production. You've actually just read the preview of one of them.

Dear friends, if you have something on your heart to do, I highly encourage you to do it. No matter what it is, with the help of the Lord, you can do it. Even if you have to start small and take one bite of the elephant at the time. I promise you'll feel a lot better about yourself if you do, not to mention, there are people waiting on you to release your fears and bring forth the gift God has placed on the inside of you.

As Nike likes to say, "Just Do It." I encourage you to go for it, you just never know where it might take you.

ONE LAST THING...

At the end of each book, I always ask, if you have enjoyed this book and believe friends and family would also enjoy it, would you be so kind to spread the word and leave me a review. I'd love to hear your thoughts, I receive all feedback, good, bad, or indifferent.

Keep in mind, no matter what your situation looks like right now, God is there, no matter what you see or feel, continue to trust in Him and trust Him completely. He promises He'll never leave you nor forsake you. I hope by now you know without a shadow of a doubt, you are **UNFORSAKEN**.

All the best,

Shakira ♥

www.ingramcontent.com/pod-product-compliance
Lightning Source LLC
Chambersburg PA
CBHW021231250626
47155CB00008B/2966